A PARTY TO MURDER

BUNTY COSGREAVE: Lady Cosgreave's daughter had a history of getting into trouble and running away from it. Was she now at it again?

★

ANNABEL HINCHBY-SMYTHE: She was the local gossip and a great fan of martinis. But the fact remained: she was the only one on Leonora's side.

★

EDDIE COSGREAVE: When Bunty's husband wasn't putting together big business deals, he was fending off murder attempts.

★

MOLLY and GILES CARMODY: The couple was the epitome of English gentry. Only one problem: for thirty years they had been married, each to someone else.

★

JAMES ABERCORN: With his pale grey eyes and nervous manners, he struck Leonora as odd—but she could not guess just how odd that really was!

★   ★   ★   ★

"Babson writes mysteries with distinctive atmosphere, sympathetic characters, and stylish verve."
—*Booklist*

Also by Marian Babson:

*Fatal Fortune**
Encore Murder

MARIAN BABSON

GUILTY PARTY

WARNER BOOKS

A Time Warner Company

WARNER BOOKS EDITION

Cover design by Jackie Merri Meyer
Cover illustration by Phillip Singer

This Warner Books Edition is published by arrangement with
St. Martin's Press, 175 Fifth Avenue, New York, N.Y. 10010

Warner Books, Inc.
1271 Avenue of the Americas
New York, NY 10020

Ⓦ A Time Warner Company

Printed in the United States of America

First Warner Books Printing: March, 1993

10 9 8 7 6 5 4 3 2 1

CHAPTER 1

Because she was essentially a kind-hearted person and because it had been a gratifyingly thick wad of currency she had carelessly (although not so carelessly that she had not kept her own mental tally while it was being counted out) swept into her handbag, Lady Cosgreave paused to offer a word of advice to her incoming tenant.

"I wouldn't mention being divorced, if I were you," she told the pale fragile girl (puff of wind would blow her away) standing before her.

"I'm not ashamed of it." Leonora's pointed chin thrust forward and upward challengingly.

"It will make life easier for you, that's all. Little Woadpit-by-Marsh is very old-fashioned, that's to say, hidebound. People will be quite interested enough, you being an American and an artist. Give them any more and they might choke on it."

"I'm not planning to get involved in the local social life," Leonora said. "I have a West End gallery willing to give me an Exhibition, if I can let them have enough pictures. I intend to shut myself away and work."

"Quite right," Lady Cosgreave approved. The child had obviously never been within a country mile of village life before. She had no idea of the amount of genteel prying she would encounter from even the most incurious inhabitant. And, as for the other tenants in and around Cosgreave Hall . . .

"But you're bound to meet with the odd question or two. Take my advice and tell them you're a widow—a recent widow. That will shut them up. Not even Annabel Hinchby-Smythe would persevere after an announcement like that."

"Why should she?" Leonora began to feel uneasy. None of these possible snags had been mentioned earlier—and now she had just handed over three months' rent in advance. "What concern is it of hers?"

"None at all, but Our Annabel is a bit of a gossip. She's quite amusing, however, and she means well . . ."

"I don't expect to meet her—or anyone else. I have far too much work to do." Leonora spoke calmly and firmly, having convinced herself that this was her only plan. She was going to bury herself in a quiet English village, where she knew no one and no one knew her. She would keep it that way. If necessary, if she were pressed, she might take Lady Cosgreave's advice and proclaim herself a widow. What was one more lie?

"You may find Annabel rather hard to avoid," Lady Cosgreave murmured. "However, I'm sure you'll manage splendidly." That it had not been an easy divorce was clear to see. The poor little thing wanted a place to hide away and lick her wounds. How very different from the divorce of her own dear Bunty, who had gone to court with a song on her lips and the millionaire stockbroker who was to become her next husband on her arm. (Something she would never have got away with in the days of the Queen's Proctor.) Of course, not everyone was possessed of Bunty's *joie de verve*, nor, indeed, her enterprise.

And Eddie was so clever . . . so very clever.

"Did you bring the keys?"

"Oh yes." Back to business. "I have them right here . . . Somewhere . . ." She rummaged through her handbag while Leonora's face took on what had to be called a sceptical expression. Such a nuisance. In the ordinary way, she'd simply have left the keys with Bunty at the Hall, but this woman and her passion for privacy . . .

"Here we are!" She surfaced triumphantly with the keys and handed them over.

"Thank you. I can't tell you how much I'm looking forward to some peace and quiet and the chance to get down to work. The past few months have been so chaotic."

"Yes, yes." The woman wasn't going to make a speech, was she? Americans took everything so seriously. Lady Cosgreave began moving towards the door, anxious to end this tedious interlude.

"I'm so grateful to you for letting me have the cottage—"

"You'll find everything you need there, including basic food supplies until you have a chance to get to the shops for yourself. I'm sure you'll be very happy there." With the end of the interview and freedom in sight, Lady Cosgreave perjured herself recklessly. "Your neighbors are charming, the loft will make a marvelous studio, and if there's anything at all you want, you can call on my daughter at Cosgreave Hall and she'll be delighted to help you. Goodbye, my dear, and the best of luck—with your painting."

CHAPTER 2

So much for good intentions.

It had started off so successfully that Leonora was subsequently unable to put her finger on just where it had all begun to go wrong.

Was it when she had failed to slam the door on the first hopeful friendly caller? But there had been something very familiar about that face; furthermore, it demanded—expected—recognition. Automatically, Leonora had opened the door.

"Good morning!" The smile was bright, even though the mouth seemed to possess several more teeth than were absolutely necessary—or desirable. "I'm Honoria—frightful name, isn't it? I can't imagine what Mummy was thinking of. Everyone calls me Bunty. Mummy told me I must check and see that you're settling in comfortably."

"Oh yes. Good morning." After that, there was nothing to do except swing the door wide and step back. You can't slam the door on the landlady's daughter. "Come in."

"Thanks awfully." There had been no doubt in her mind that she would be welcome. She strode into the tiny hallway and looked around, tossing her head. "You haven't made any changes yet, I see."

"I don't plan to. I just want a place to work."

"So Mummy said. You're Canadian, aren't you?"

"American."

"I knew it would be one or the other." Bunty gave a careless shrug and walked past her into the living-room. "Mummy always insists on it."

"Does she?" The news was a surprise. Lady Cosgreave had not struck Leonora as an enthusiastic exponent of Hands Across the Sea—or of anything else. The only moment when Her Ladyship had shown any emotion warmer than indifference was when she had put the rent money away in her handbag.

"And you haven't moved a thing in here—" Bunty hurled herself down on the sofa and looked around with a proprietorial gaze. *Not even to dust* hung in the air.

"I've only been here a few days—" Leonora was annoyed to find herself on the defensive.

"Don't worry, we'll get you organized," Bunty said decisively. "Old Ruby will take you on. I'll speak to her about it. Twice a week, she used to come here and clean; she can fit you right back into her schedule."

"That's very kind of you, but I'm not sure I want anyone. I have a lot of work to do and I don't want to be disturbed—"

"Oh, that's no problem. She has her own keys and she can come and go without bothering you at all. She'll be delighted to help out. I suspect she's been feeling the draught since the Ordways left."

"The Ordways used to live here?"

"Not for long. They were Canadians—" Bunty gave a snort of laughter. "They couldn't stand the strain of country life."

Perhaps there was an answer to that, but Leonora didn't know it. There was something uncomfortably insinuating about Bunty's laughter: there was a private joke here somewhere. Outsiders were not expected to recognize the joke—or even to realize that there was one.

"Have you—" Bunty abruptly reverted to business—"notified the post office that you're living here now?"

"Not yet." Leonora wasn't expecting any letters, but something told her that it might not be wise to mention this.

"I thought not!" Bunty was triumphant. "You haven't a clue, have you? Never mind, that's why Mummy sent me along. We'll have you in the swing of things in no time!"

"But I—" Before she could say that she didn't want to be in the swing of things, Bunty had leaped to her feet.

"You'll like it here!" There was no room for argument. "Yes—" Bunty ran her eyes over Leonora—a general inspecting his troops. "I know you will."

Leonora was miserably aware that the troops didn't pass muster. Bunty was wearing the traditional English country uniform of cashmere twinset, tweed skirt and pearls. Her own skirt was of some composition material with several pulled threads; she could only be thankful that her nylon sweater was concealed by a paint-smeared smock. She had not bothered with jewelry at all.

Nevertheless, Lady Cosgreave's daughter seemed not unpleased.

"Sunday morning—elevenish—come up to the Hall for drinks!" It was more of an order than an invitation.

"Thank you, but—" Leonora followed her to the front door.

"And you're not to bother dressing up—" Bunty issued another order, her gaze resting complacently on a large hole in the calf of Leonora's tights. "You're fine just the way you are. You'll fit right in."

It took all the restraint she possessed, but Leonora managed not to slam the door behind her departing guest. Did the idiot woman think she would actually turn up for drinks dressed in her painting outfit? Or did Bunty imagine that she possessed no better clothes?

As her annoyance mounted, Leonora found that she was automatically planning her outfit for Sunday's gathering. She was so determined to show Bunty that ragamuffinery was not her usual state that she had already forgotten her resolve to retreat into her work and live the life of a recluse.

CHAPTER 3

Everything considered, Leonora had thought she was doing quite well at keeping up her side of the small talk. The weather, past, present and probable future, had been covered exhaustively. The scenery, the village shops and the best nearby towns for shopping and historic buildings had also been given due assessment. Emboldened, she had tried to extend the conversation and suddenly it had all gone wrong.

The pale well-bred face froze, eyebrows and moustache twitched in unison and went still. The pale grey eyes glazed and shifted from her face to stare desperately over her shoulder, seeking rescue. What had been so terrible about her harmless remark?

"What a beautiful old house this is." That was all she had said, adding, "I've always wanted to see inside of one of these glorious old Elizabethan manor houses."

That was when James Abercorn, retired History Master living in a converted flat over what had been the stables, had twitched and gone into his impersonation of a dead carp.

"How're you doing?" Rescue was at hand. Eddie, the genial host, appeared with a pitcher of martinis. "Let me top you up."

"No, thanks, old man." James spoke before Leonora could. "I've reached my limit, I'm afraid. Any more—" He laughed, suddenly amiable and social again. "Any more, and I shan't answer for the consequences."

"Yeah, right. Okay." Eddie did an abrupt about-face and went over to another group, leaving Leonora with her glass still extended. Rudeness? Cheapness? Or was he merely the sort of male chauvinist who took the answer of a man to apply to his female companion, also? When she knew her host better, she might be able to decide, but she did not look forward to getting to know him better—and that went for James Abercorn, as well.

"Mmm, yes . . ." James Abercorn swirled the remaining inch of fluid about in his glass and looked at her with no more enthusiasm than she felt for him. "This house—" He darted a guilty look at his host's back. "It, er, it isn't genuine, you know."

Leonora smiled tightly. If she had known, she wouldn't have made the remark. Had he gone into shock because of her ignorance, or because he had seen the host heading towards them and didn't want to risk correcting her when he might be overheard? She was beginning to wish that she had skipped this party, after all.

Yet it had started quite promisingly. Bunty had been properly chagrined to see her properly attired, with no lingering trace of the ragamuffin look. There had even been a moment of flattering reluctance to introduce Leonora to Eddie. Propriety had won, however, and the introduction had been made. Bunty's relief had been almost palpable when she realized that, despite being fellow Americans, they had no interest in each other.

Greatly cheered by this, Bunty had then steered Leonora to another group—on the far side of the drawing-room —and made further introductions before leaving her with them.

Molly and Giles Carmody ("The Colonel and his Lady," Bunty had trilled) had been charming and slightly self-deprecating.

"Retired Colonel, actually," Giles had said.

"And depends what you call a lady," Molly quietly mocked. "You've probably gathered by now that Bunty isn't always accurate."

They had all laughed companionably, secure in their position, sharing the joke about their hostess.

"You've taken over the old gardener's cottage, I believe," Molly said. "Not that there's been a gardener there recently. They have some sort of landscaping contract now with a firm in town who come out about three times a year and replant the flowerbeds so there's always an impressive floral display. Between times, the rest of us take it in turn to do the odd bit of dead-heading and weeding."

"We occupy the East Wing," Giles said. "They've made it into rather a decent sort of maisonette."

"I see." Leonora was beginning to. "And are all the people here, um, residents?"

"Do you know—" Molly looked around—"I believe they are. I hadn't noticed that before. It's quite a parochial little gathering this morning."

"And here's the West Wing." Molly smiled at a short dark-haired woman who had just drifted up to join them. "Clio Warriner, have you met Leonora Rice? She's the new tenant in the gardener's cottage."

"How do you do?" Clio smiled warmly, if vaguely. "I'm afraid I hadn't noticed anyone had moved in. There's always so much to do before Tom gets back from one of his business trips. In fact—" she frowned slightly—"I'd never have managed it all if he weren't late. He should have been home a couple of days ago—"

"Slipped the leash again, has he?" Giles's chortle was cut short as Molly's elbow landed in his ribs.

"I don't really have time for socializing," Leonora said quickly. "I have so much work to do that I grudge the time I spend going to the shops."

"Ah well," Giles said. "You're talking to the right person now. Our Clio has all the shopkeepers in the palm of her hand. They actually make deliveries for her. We're all trying to discover her secret method for controlling them."

"Nonsense," Clio said. "I never ask for special privileges. They'd do the same for anyone."

"Ah, what it is to be siren." Giles eyed Leonora speculatively. "And you've the makings of one yourself, I'd say. The two of you would make a formidable duo. Heaven help a poor shopkeeper when you roll those eyes at him."

"Actually," Clio said graciously to Leonora, "if you'd like, I'll take you round and introduce you to the best of the local shops. And there are a couple of very good department stores just a few miles from here—"

Molly nudged Giles again and they slipped off in the direction of a woman who had just come in. "We leave you in excellent hands, then . . ." Molly murmured.

"We could organize an excursion any day you like," Clio went on relentlessly. "Just say the word."

"Perhaps I could let you know later," Leonora evaded. "I'm still getting settled in—and I *do* have a lot of work to do." Perhaps, if she said it often enough, it might register.

"Of course, I quite understand," Clio sounded disappointed. "We'll get together later and arrange something."

"That will be fine." Unaccountably, Leonora felt guilty.

"James, dear—" Clio greeted another latecomer. "I'd wondered if you were coming. Have you met . . . ?"

Introductions were duly made and, after a few more desultory remarks, Clio moved off to speak to her hostess.

That was when Leonora, left by herself with James Abercorn, made her first *faux pas*.

* * *

"Oh yes." Unwittingly, she embarked on her second. "The house has been restored, you mean?" She remembered the books she had read before coming over here. "Rebuilt after the original had been destroyed by bombs during the war?"

"Er . . . no, not exactly." Once more, his face was immobile, while his eyes rolled wildly, seeking someone who would deliver him from this idiot.

Another pitcher of martinis wafted forward. James thrust out his empty glass so that it clinked against the side of the pitcher, stopping the woman carrying it dead in her tracks.

"Hello, James." Her bright blue eyes assessed his frozen face. "Yes," she decided, "it does look as though your need is greater than mine." Expertly, she refilled his glass to the brim.

"Thanks most awfully," he babbled. "Er, you know what's-her-name here, don't you? New neighbour—" He gulped deeply, then, clutching his glass, he escaped.

"What have you been saying to upset James?" The amused gaze focused on Leonora. "Not that it takes much."

"He seems very shy," Leonora said defensively.

"That, too," the woman agreed. "His sort are always more comfortable with a classroom full of young boys than with a full-blooded woman. Oh, don't misunderstand," she said quickly. "Nothing like that. He's just a severe case of arrested development. So many of them are."

"Schoolmaster, you mean?" Leonora found that she was able to follow this turn of conversation reasonably well.

"Among others." Absently, the woman refilled her own glass. "Oh, sorry, let me—" She topped up Leonora's glass.

"Thank you." Leonora did not expect to be told that she was welcome and, sure enough, the woman remained silent. In fact, she was gazing at the depleted level of her pitcher with an expression that suggested the opposite.

The woman was tall and thin as a scarecrow; generous draperies fluttered on her spare frame. Her sleek silver hair was cut in what was once called a Dutch Bob. Pinpoints of light darted from dangling diamonds on her earlobes, the choker around her throat, and at least three fingers on each hand.

Leonora was momentarily bemused: if she wore this for a morning sherry party, what did she wear for a formal dinner? Not, Leonora realized, that she had yet seen any sherry being served. Martinis seemed to be the order of the day, perhaps out of deference to Bunty's American husband.

"Dinah told me to look out for you." The woman had not stopped talking. "You're the artist, aren't you? The—" her gaze raked Leonora's little black dress—"the young widow?"

"Oh . . . yes." So Lady Cosgreave was going to do her lying for her, was she? Didn't she trust Leonora to do it for herself? But—had the hesitation been too long?

It had. She saw a beady look sharpen the blue eyes; behind them, a suspicion flared and was filed for future reference.

"I know I upset Mr. Abercorn." Leonora threw it out quickly, hoping it would provide a distraction. "But I don't know what I said wrong."

"Practically anything would do it," her companion said. "Unlike most of the people around here, James is a sensitive soul. What were you discussing?"

"This lovely old house—"

"Old? This?" She gave a hoot of derision. "If you called this old, no wonder he was upset. No—don't tell me! Did you really think it was Elizabethan?"

"Well, yes . . ."

"Hah! It's just a nasty Victorian fake. They were besotted by the Tudor image, you know. Dinah's great-grandfather built it to commemorate successfully buying his title. There was a lot of money in the family then. They're the sort who used to be called the Landed Gentry; nowadays, with taxes, death duties and all that, they're known as the Stranded Gentry.

"House got much too big for them to cope with after the Second World War when they couldn't get servants any more—not for what they could afford to pay. By then, half of it needed rebuilding. Family offered it to the National Trust, who laughed in their faces. It was falling to bits when, fortunately, Bunty latched on to Eddie. He patched up the worst of it and leased off the wings on full repairing leases and they've never looked back. You're not on a repairing lease, are you?''

"No, I'm on a simple quarterly tenancy."

"Keep it that way. Don't let them talk you into anything more complicated or you'll live to regret it! Oh-oh!'' She looked across the room to where Clio Warriner stood alone, looking forlorn. Clio had just set down her glass and picked up a glass paperweight, peering at it abstractedly, as though trying to read the future in it.

"Excuse me. I must just have a word with Clio."

She moved off, leaving Leonora stunned and exhausted and with the inescapable feeling that she had just met Annabel Hinchby-Smythe.

CHAPTER 4

Next morning, Leonora realized that it had been a tactical error to go to the sherry party. Her neighbours had taken her appearance as a signal that she was available for social activities and the first telephone call had come at nine o'clock, just as she was finishing breakfast and looking forward to a morning at the easel.

"Good morning, it's Clio Warriner here." The voice was high and nervous. "I hope it isn't too early to ring?"

"No, it's all right." Leonora gave the expected reassurance with some foreboding, but she could not be rude when Clio was making a friendly overture. Later, she would mention that the best time to telephone was in the evening. It always took a while to train strangers not to waste her time during the precious daylight hours.

"Oh, good. I wanted to catch you before the others did. You were saying that you'd like to do some shopping. I thought we might go sometime this week. Tomorrow, perhaps, or Wednesday? Thursday is half-day closing, so that isn't so good. Friday and Saturday are market days and they're rather a bun fight, although it might amuse you . . . ?"

"Oh yes . . ." Leonora vaguely remembered agreeing to a

shopping tour of the district. She hadn't expected to be offered it so soon. Of course, she did need some proper lighting and the sooner, the better. Sacrificing a few hours of daylight now would mean that she could continue to work after dark in the future.

"Perhaps you'd prefer next week . . . ?" Clio sounded downcast; she'd obviously hoped for more enthusiasm.

"No, this week will be fine. My first priority is some decent lighting. If you know of a good electrical store where I can pick up a couple of spotlights and a floor lamp and a supply of bulbs—"

"Anselm's Department Store," Clio said firmly, evidently on home ground. "They're the best. They even have that special lighting that's supposed to counteract depression. There was an article in the paper about it a few weeks ago. It's supposed to be better than daylight."

"Oh yes, I've heard of that." She wasn't sure how it would affect paint colors, but it was definitely worth investigating.

"Tomorrow, then?" Clio suggested eagerly.

"Well, Wednesday would be better for me. If that's all right with you."

"Oh . . . yes. That will be all right." Clio sounded a trifle disappointed.

"That will give me a chance to have a good look around and see what else I need here. I'll probably have quite a shopping list by the time I've finished."

"Oh, I quite understand," Clio said. "It's always *so* difficult moving into a rented place, isn't it? Tom and I had quite a few years of it when we were starting out. Things are never quite the way you'd like them. It always takes such ages to get things into your own sort of order."

"That's right." Leonora decided not to admit that she had no intention of worrying about order to that extent. All she required was a minimum of comfort and space, with a maximum of light, materials, and peace and quiet—especially peace and quiet.

"I'll call by for you Wednesday morning, then," Clio said uneasily, as though the unspoken thought had reached her.

"Fine," Leonora said firmly. "I'll see you then."

The next telephone call was from Molly Carmody.

"I hope I'm not disturbing you. I know you're frightfully busy . . ." Molly's voice had the inbuilt guilt of one who realized her favored position as a woman who did not need to work to support herself.

"That's all right." Leonora gave the expected reply again, grinding her teeth only slightly. "I have a moment now. What is it?"

"We're having a little bridge party on Thursday. Do say you'll come. All work and no play, you know—"

"Sorry, I can't play bridge."

"You can't play?" Molly was incredulous. "You mean you don't know how?"

"I never learned," Leonora said crisply. One of the most useful tips she had received at art school had been from the teacher (female, of course) who had, from the depths of her own experience, earnestly advised all female art students to avoid learning any card games at all. It had preserved many an afternoon for her work.

"Oh! Well, we could teach you . . . or, perhaps, we could play whist." As all prospective hostesses did, Molly was rallying. "Or canasta?"

"Sorry, no card games at all," Leonora said blithely. "And I can't learn. It's hopeless. I'm one of the 'Who led that slice of salami?' school. You wouldn't want me. I'd only ruin the game for the others."

"Oh well . . ." Molly was routed. "Perhaps another time . . . when we aren't playing bridge . . ."

"That will be fine." Leonora rang off before Molly could launch into any more counter-proposals.

After that, she had a clear half-hour to herself before she

became aware that someone was moving about on the ground floor. She went to the head of the stairs and listened. It was unlikely that burglars were operating in this village. She began to descend the stairs silently. It was far more likely to be the cleaning woman . . .

A stairboard creaked sharply.

"Hello-ello-ello—" Carolling brightly, Bunty appeared in the living-room doorway, trying to look as though she had just arrived and glanced into the living-room in search of Leonora.

"Oh, *there* you are," she said accusingly. "I've been looking everywhere for you. I didn't wake you, did I?" She made it sound as though she had been calling out since she had entered the house.

"No, I've been up for hours. I've been working." Leonora decided not to take issue with Bunty right now, but made a mental note to add a doorchain to her shopping list. The terms of her rental agreement most definitely did not include allowing the landlady's daughter to roam through her quarters at will.

"Oh, good. I'm glad I didn't disturb you." Bunty turned and led the way back into the living-room, automatically assuming the role of hostess. "You're settling in well, I trust?"

"I'm trying to." Leonora remained standing while Bunty sank into the armchair beside the fireplace.

"You made a great hit at the party," Bunty assured her complacently. "But then, I knew you would. You must come again—and stay for lunch next time. Eddie often has American colleagues down for the weekend. You'd enjoy meeting them." It sounded like an order.

"I probably would . . . sometime. When I haven't so much work on hand . . ." Leonora leaned against the door-jamb and let the silence lengthen. Casually, she glanced around the room and noticed distinct signs that papers had been disturbed on the *secretaire* in the corner. And one drawer had not been completely closed . . . although she had left it closed.

"Well . . ." Bunty followed the direction of her gaze and leaped to her feet abruptly. "I must get back. No rest for the wicked."

"Yes," Leonora said, still pointedly staring at the protruding drawer.

"Bye for now." Bunty nearly tripped over her own feet, rushing for the door.

Leonora stood aside and let her pass, then followed her and shut the front door firmly behind her.

After that, she promised herself that she would not answer the telephone or the doorbell for the rest of the day, but, as it turned out, she had no need to. It seemed that the flurry of friendliness had petered out. Or perhaps word had gone round that she was not so welcoming as might be hoped. She was left undisturbed for the remainder of the day.

It was not until the light had died away that she stepped back from the blurring canvas, stretched, and realized that she was hungry, exhausted and her back ached. She washed her hands, then went downstairs to the kitchen, turned on the inadequate light (of a wattage so low it seemed to add to the twilight gloom instead of dispelling it) and looked in the fridge to see what she could turn into a quick meal.

The refrigerator light was brighter than the kitchen light, but that was about all that could be said for the refrigerator. Eggs again, there wasn't much else. Lady Cosgreave's idea of what constituted adequate supplies did not coincide with her own. For a fleeting moment she regretted having postponed the shopping trip with Clio until the day after tomorrow, but it was more important to get on with her work. A couple of days of scrambled eggs, boiled eggs and omelettes wouldn't kill her.

The kettle had not yet boiled before there was a knock at the back door. Opening it, she found Annabel Hinchby-Smythe standing there with a covered plate in one hand and a pitcher of clear liquid, possibly lemonade, in the other.

"Time for tea," Annabel announced. "I've heard you're not in the mood for visiting today, so I thought I'd bring the tea to you instead of the other way round. You don't want to get dressed up and go out, but now that the light's gone, you're ready for a bit of socializing, aren't you?"

"Yes." Leonora discovered that she was. She opened the door wider. "Come in. How kind of you."

"Think nothing of it!" Annabel swept in, deposited her offerings on the kitchen table and turned off the gas as the kettle began to sing. "We won't need that for a while," she said dismissively.

"We won't?" Leonora felt the first qualm. Annabel, in her own way, could obviously be quite as high-handed as the land-lady's daughter. She wondered if she had made a mistake in being so welcoming.

But nothing was what it seemed. Annabel whipped the napkin off the plate of sandwiches to reveal substantial brown triangles well-filled with corned beef-and-cheese ce-mented with a layer of crunchy piccalilli, rather than the delicate white bread and cucumber sandwiches she had expected.

As for the lemonade—she should have known better. Leonora choked on the first gulp and gasped for air. It was a martini—full American strength, almost pure gin barely tainted by the merest hint of dry vermouth.

"Oh!" she choked. "That was stronger than I expected." She did not add that she had been expecting lemonade.

"Learned to make proper martinis when I was living in the States," Annabel said proudly. "You don't often get them like that in this country."

"You certainly don't." Unobtrusively, Leonora wiped her streaming eyes.

"Of course," Annabel added thoughtfully, "one has to be rather careful about who one serves them to."

Leonora smiled, deciding that it would be churlish at this

point to ask to be listed among the unappreciative. Perhaps, when she knew Annabel better . . .

"These sandwiches are very good," she said instead.

"I didn't think you'd have a lot in the larder, knowing Bunty." Annabel raised an inquiring eyebrow.

"Oh, there are plenty of eggs," Leonora said quickly, not wishing to seem critical.

"Are there?" Annabel had no such qualms. She crossed to the fridge, opened the door and inspected the contents. "Just as I thought—size 5 eggs! The only ones smaller are quails' eggs—and she wouldn't give you those. They're too expensive."

"Honestly, I don't mind. I quite like eggs and it's only for a couple of days. Clio is taking me shopping Wednesday and I'll stock up properly then."

Annabel looked at her doubtfully for a long moment, then sighed and shrugged. "Oh well, I suppose it will be all right."

"I don't mind," Leonora assured her. "I'd rather do my own shopping anyway. All I needed these first few days was just a little something to keep me going—"

"And that was what you got," Annabel said wryly. "As little as possible. Oh, don't misunderstand—" She held up a disclaiming hand. "I'm quite fond of Bunty, really. We all are. It's just that we're used to her little ways and you're not. Not yet."

"She drops in unexpectedly, I've learned that this morning," Leonora said. "Also, she doesn't bother to ring the doorbell. Do you think it would be unforgivable if I were to have the locks changed?"

"Mmm . . . might be awkward. Leave it with me. I'll have a quiet word with her. Just knowing that you're thinking of such a thing might do the trick."

"I hope so. I don't like the idea of her walking into the place whenever she feels like it."

"Can't blame you for that. Not many people *would* want Our Bunty barging in on them. What was her excuse? She usually has some flimsy pretext when she's being especially outrageous."

"Oh, something about was I settling in well. And something else, rather vague, about going to another drinks party and lunch next time Eddie has some American friends down."

"That'll be it, then. Dear Eddie seems to be bringing half the City home with him these Friday nights. And Bunty likes to have the residents turn out on parade to amuse her weekend guests. She'll want you to be there, too—now that you've passed muster."

"Passed muster?"

"You dressed well enough, spoke well enough—and didn't make a pass at Eddie. That's all that's required. You've now joined the rest of us on the guest list for all occasions—particularly those when Eddie's wheeler-dealer American friends are present."

Leonora had begun to laugh before she realized that Annabel was perfectly serious.

"It's also quite likely," Annabel said thoughtfully, "that she wanted to make sure you weren't a Merry Widow. She likes to have all the attention from wealthy male guests to herself. Competition upsets her."

"Oh?" This was a new light on Bunty. A somewhat disquieting light. "I hadn't thought she was, er, flirtatious."

"You could pitch it stronger than that. I would." Annabel poured herself another drink and promptly did. "Gel's a Bolter. Old-fashioned word, perhaps, but the type never goes out of fashion. Bolts. Long record of it. Bolted from boarding school with the under-gardener. Luckily, they caught up with her before she could get him to a Registry Office. School wouldn't take her back, of course. Dinah was livid because they wouldn't refund that term's fees, either. They said the other side had violated the contract and now they'd have to find a new under-gardener, as well. Couldn't take him back, either. Were afraid he'd acquired a taste for young heiresses—and discovered how easy they were to acquire. Couldn't have that. Parents would have taken their daughters away, once word got out. Nothing more vulnerable than a school.''

"Good heavens,'' Leonora said faintly.

"That was just the start of it,'' Annabel went on with relish. "After that, it was just one bolt after another with whatever likely lad was nearest to hand. No hairdresser was safe. Three schools washed their hands of her and she was sent down from University. Dinah breathed a sigh of relief when she finally got her to the altar with Gerald—the first husband. He wasn't too bright, of course, but he had money and was in line for a title. Didn't wait about for him to inherit, though. Dear Eddie came along—another mug—with pots more money. Even Dinah approved.''

"They seem very happy together.'' It wasn't much of a comment, but it was the best Leonora could do. Already, she was wondering just how she could look Bunty in the eye again, now that she knew of her colorful past.

"Hah! *He* thinks so, poor idiot! If you ask me, she's looking round again. I've caught that glimpse in her eye. Oh, Eddie is rich, all right, but some of those business prospects he keeps entertaining are *mega*rich. Don't think she hasn't noticed that!''

"No, please.'' Leonora tried to retract her glass as Annabel levelled the pitcher over it and was liberally splashed for her pains.

"Can't fly on one wing! That's what I learned in the War. We all drank as though there was no tomorrow. There wasn't—for a lot of us. Old habits die hard. Chin-chin!'' Annabel disposed of her own drink and poured herself another.

Leonora sipped at her drink. It wasn't too bad, once you got used to it. In view of Annabel's conversation, the strength was welcome. Did the woman gossip so uninhibitedly about every-

one? Not that it mattered. She hadn't planned on confiding in
Annabel, anyway.

Outside, the sound of an automobile motor grew louder as a
car approached through the gateposts. Annabel dashed to the
window and twitched aside the curtain, peering out avidly.

"Giles," she reported. "And Molly isn't with him.
Mmm . . . I wonder . . . ?" She turned away from the window
briskly.

"Must go now. See you tomorrow."

She was out of the door and heading for the East Wing
before Leonora had a chance to reply. She had left the now-
depleted pitcher of martinis and empty sandwich plate behind
her, which meant, Leonora realized glumly, that they probably
would see each other tomorrow because it would be necessary
to return the plate and pitcher.

CHAPTER 5

Leonora woke just before dawn with a raging thirst, a throbbing head and a growing determination never to drink another martini. In Annabel's bejewelled grasp, a cocktail shaker became a lethal weapon.

She was on her second glass of water when she realized the throbbing wasn't all in her head. With a dexterity that equalled Annabel's, she simultaneously switched off the light and twitched aside the curtain in time to see a long, low, black car turn in from the street and zoom up the driveway.

An unlikely hour for visitors, surely?

Someone returning home, then? A distinct possibility. Even as she watched, the headlights went out and the car proceeded at a slower pace using only its sidelights. Then the motor cut out and the car coasted the last few yards around to the side of the Hall where the garages were located.

Definitely someone returning home. What kind of car did Giles have? This dark sleek monster seemed too high-powered for him, somehow. Perhaps . . .

Her head gave an almighty throb, reminding her that she was not Annabel and that she had problems of her own. She let

27

the curtain fall back into place, put the dim light on again and resumed her fruitless search of the medicine cabinet for aspirins.

Morning was well advanced when she awoke again. Cautious movements established that she was functional, although it would be unwise to get too ambitious. A slow crawl to the kitchen and coffee and toast would just about shoot her bolt for the next few hours.

Her stomach lurched unexpectedly. Well, just coffee, then. Perhaps orange juice, if she took it very slowly.

She turned on the radio and lowered the sound to a murmur. She discovered that the day was to go on as it had begun: grey, misty and dull, with the possibility of heavy rain before nightfall. A good day to stay in and work—or would be, if she had any decent artificial lighting.

As it was, perhaps she just might do a few pencil sketches for another project that had been at the back of her mind for some time now. After so many years of illustrating children's books, she thought she might try her hand at doing the whole book by herself. Oh, nothing too ambitious, more illustration than text, but a start. She had thought for a long time that she'd like to have a try, but Paul had always jeered at the idea.

Paul . . . how long had he been quietly denigrating her talents, belittling her, undermining her confidence, before she had become aware of it?

Longer than it should have been. It had started so innocently—as a joke—and continued so insidiously, that it had become an entrenched part of their relationship before she had realized what was happening.

Little Leonora with her little gift for amusing the little ones. Paul, of course, worked in the "real" world where he already had managerial status and was tipped for the top echelon, probably before he reached forty. Yet, somehow, it never quite seemed to happen. There was always someone blocking his way, someone he had alienated and who was "getting back" at him by blocking his promotion.

Gradually, regretfully, Leonora had begun to recognize that Paul was one of these people who had never learned that you cannot build up yourself by tearing down others. As he found himself increasingly frustrated in his own career, he had lashed out at those around him. Unfortunately, she had been the nearest. It had been a long and painful process of destruction.

The moment of truth had come at Laura's dinner party. Paul had had a bad day (another one) at the office and was in a surly mood. Knowing that it would only make things worse, she had not reminded him that it was publication day for her new book.

Laura had remembered. For dessert, she had served a cake in the shape of an open book with a rough copy of one of the illustrations in icing. Whereupon, with whoops of glee, the other guests had each produced a copy of the book and merrily insisted on autographs.

Laughing and signing the books, Leonora had looked up unexpectedly and caught the expression on Paul's face.

I'll pay for this later. The thought—fully formed for the first time—made her shudder involuntarily. And yet she recognized that it had been lying dormant in her subconscious for a long while.

For the rest of the evening, in front of Laura and her guests, Paul had concentrated on being charming. Leonora could no longer be fooled so easily. Numb with apprehension, she waited for the blow to fall.

She hadn't long to wait. Back in their apartment, Paul stumbled and, in a clumsy flailing movement, swept her treasured porcelain collection off the mantelpiece to crash upon the hearth.

"I'm sorry," he said, regaining his balance with an air of satisfaction. "I tripped. It was an accident."

"Strange," she said, "the way *your* accidents always break *my* things."

"What the hell do you mean by that?" he blustered.

"Just what I said." She could hear her own voice, cold and distant. She could see that something in her expression was unsettling Paul.

"I told you it was an accident. I'm sorry." Perhaps, this time, he could see that he had gone too far. "I'll replace them. I'll get you better ones." He moved towards her.

"Don't bother." She moved away. "I don't want any more. I think I've outgrown such things."

And outgrown you. There was pain in the realization. They had had some good years, but the good times had been fewer and farther apart lately.

"You're upset," he said, looking frightened, as though he had heard the unspoken message. "You're overtired and upset. I'll make it up to you."

"There's nothing more you can do." She knew now why she had never pressed for marriage, never wanted Paul's child. She had even refused to have a pet when Paul had proposed getting her one. Not a dog, cat or canary—no hostages to fortune. Nothing alive and able to be hurt that Paul could use against her.

"It's been a long day," he said. "Let's go to bed."

"Later. I want to clear up here first. You go ahead."

Paul was asleep when she looked in on him. She had spent the rest of the night sitting up in the armchair, thinking.

After Paul left in the morning, still apologetic, promising her a nice surprise when he came home, she had packed her belongings and walked out. The time had come to cut her losses.

But it had not been that easy. Paul had discovered her new address and pursued her with cryptic notes and telephone calls, unable to believe that he had destroyed their relationship, that she had finally seen through his machinations.

Even so, she had still been surprised to discover how much she had lost without noticing. The friends—her friends—he had alienated with mocking, disparaging remarks. The self-confidence that was so much more tentative and fragile than it had been before Paul. The self-reliance that she was having to learn all over again.

The rebuilding process was not helped by Paul's constant harassment. He refused to give up, even though he already had a new victim in his sights. Someone as trusting and innocent as she had once been. A child so gullible she had added her telephone calls to his, berating Leonora for her cold-heartedness and boasting of how much more happiness she was giving to poor bruised Paul.

Leonora had listened silently and then hung up. It would not be long before the new love found out who wound up bruised when there was a difference of opinion with poor Paul.

Leonora had changed her telephone number for one that was unlisted (ex-Directory, they said in this country) but the calls had continued, sometimes endless haranguing, sometimes after-midnight silent menace. She realized that it had become part of a delightful new game Paul had devised for his new love and that stronger steps were necessary to escape the situation.

In the end, it was the very fact that Paul had lost her so many of her friends that made it easier for her. If she had to start all over again anyway, it would not be much more difficult to start in a different country; escape the net altogether. Paul was essentially too lazy to try to trace her beyond the Continental boundaries, and too parsimonious to use the telephone for harassment at International Rates. He and his new love could turn their undivided attention to each other—and see how long the honeymoon would last.

At least she had not been fool enough to marry him. It was ironic that she had decided that a divorce would sound more respectable to Lady Cosgreave than a broken love-affair and Lady Cosgreave had, despite her daughter's record, decreed that widowhood was an even more respectable state.

Her coffee was cold and the toast protruded from the toaster, also cold.

As cold as the past—which *was* past.

Leonora pushed herself away from the table and stood up, resolutely ignoring one last vagrant twinge of pain. If she allowed herself to sit here brooding any longer, she would have wasted the morning, perhaps wasted the whole day. And that meant Paul would have won. She had not come this far to let him defeat her now.

The threatened rain never arrived (falling on some other area, perhaps), so Leonora was able to work on a painting until the light faded. Then she carried her sketchbook down into the living-room, switched on the electric fire and curled up in a corner of the sofa, tilting the shade of the lamp on the end table so that the maximum light fell upon the page. It was more of a glow than a light and Leonora reminded herself again that it was just as well that she had agreed to let Clio drive her to the shops tomorrow; at least a dozen high-wattage light-bulbs were required to bring the house up to a satisfactory standard, and it would be as well to keep another dozen on hand as spares.

There was no problem about the strength of the electric fire, however, especially after she had switched on all three bars and the blower. The warmth spread out to encompass the entire room, the last vestige of daylight expired outside the windows and she was alone in a world of her own, ideas flowing. At first, she did meticulous drawings, then rough sketches as the ideas tumbled over each other.

She was unaware of the exact point at which sleep overcame her and ideas transmuted into fantastic dreams. As was the case with dreams, every progression seemed logical and inevitable. She slid from conscious reality into unconscious fantasy, down a slope of beautiful multi-coloured ever-changing patterns, any of which would have made exquisite wallpaper, fabric designs or delicate pieces of jewellery, if only she had been able to halt the fast-flowing images long enough to sketch them and capture them.

Her sketchbook slid from her lap to the rug, landing so softly that it did not intrude upon her dreams. Her pencil followed it as her head tipped back against the cushions . . .

She awoke abruptly with pins and needles in her feet, a cramp in her shoulders and the disquieting feeling that something was very wrong.

She blinked and stared around her, momentarily disorientated. At first, she thought the sounds had come from the fire, then remembered that it was an electric fire—completely soundless. Nor was there anything else in the room that might be making those funny crunching noises; perhaps they had been a particularly vivid part of an unremembered dream.

As she sat up and slid her feet into her shoes, she heard them again. This time she was able to recognize that they were coming from outside the house.

Immediately outside. On the gravel path surrounding the cottage. Footsteps. A prowler.

City-bred, street-wise, she doused the light instantly. Now only the glow from the electric fire lit the room; it was enough to see by. In the darkness, she moved across to the window, mentally berating herself. She should have drawn the curtains as soon as it began to get dark, but she hadn't planned to fall asleep. She had thought she had time to enjoy watching the daylight fade outside the window.

Now her watch told her it was two o'clock in the morning; she was alone in a strange house in a strange country—and there was a prowler outside. She wondered how well Annabel's bonhomie would stand up to a 2:00 a.m. telephone call for help.

At the thought of Annabel, some of her equilibrium returned. Annabel—and all the others. She was not alone in the midst of the country. There were plenty of people occupying the Manor house and its surrounding cottages. Someone might be taking a walk around the grounds, never dreaming they were alarming their newest neighbor.

There was no one in view from the window now, nor any sound of further footsteps, although that might only mean that someone had stepped off the path and on to the grass.

On the other hand, perhaps he had simply gone home to bed. There was a lighted window in the turret over the front door of Cosgreave Hall, proving that she was not the only one awake at this hour.

Vaguely comforted, she listened again to the silence, then drew the curtains and went back to the sofa. She switched on the lamp and retrieved her sketchbook from the floor. Glancing through it, she was pleasantly surprised at how much she had accomplished before sleep had overtaken her. If she could continue at this rate, she would be finished a lot sooner than she had thought.

She felt a glow of exhilaration. The gamble she had taken in moving down here to this quiet cottage was paying off already. An early start in the morning—

She had almost forgotten. Tomorrow she had promised to go shopping with Clio. Now she was ready to begrudge every moment she would have to spend away from her easel and sketchpad.

Perhaps she could postpone the shopping trip. Telephone Clio first thing in the morning with apologies and suggest another day.

CHAPTER 6

In the event, Clio was at the door before Leonora had time to wonder whether she really had enough courage to telephone her and postpone their shopping trip. Looking into Clio's expectant face, she could not do it now and resigned herself to the expedition.

"I'm not too early, am I?" Clio beamed at her. "It's such a lovely day, I thought we'd take full advantage of it. We'll drive direct to Highmarsh and start at Anselm's, then I know a lovely little country pub where we can have lunch. Then you really ought to see a few of the local beauty spots—you might want to paint them. Then, if we have time before they close, we can do some of the local shops."

"Fine." It was an ambitious program and clearly Clio had devoted considerable enthusiasm to planning it. Leonora could not be so churlish as to cavil. She forced a smile. "Would you like a cup of coffee before we start?"

"No, thank you. Let's not hang about. Anselm's has a divine penthouse restaurant and this is the sort of day when they'll be serving morning coffee on the terrace. We can have it there."

"That sounds very nice." Having resigned herself to a lost

day, Leonora determined to enjoy it. "Just let me get my shopping list and my jacket and I'm ready."

Clio was an excellent driver and obviously took great delight in having a passenger with whom to share the journey and her pleasure in the sights along the way.

Leonora could not help remembering Giles Carmody's comment about Clio's elusive husband and wondered if Clio were often lonely. It had sounded, in retrospect, as though Clio might be a neglected wife, perhaps unappreciated, disparaged. In which case, they had more in common than might have been apparent at first.

"We'll soon be there," Clio said encouragingly.

"Oh, sorry." Leonora realized that she had just sighed aloud. "It's not the company—or the journey. I just haven't been sleeping too well lately."

"Strange beds." Clio nodded sagely. "I hate travel myself and moving to new places. It unsettles one for so long afterwards."

"And strange noises," Leonora said tentatively.

"Oh, definitely!" Clio nodded again. "Strange noises are even worse than strange beds—and new places are always alive with strange noises. Especially country places . . . if you aren't used to living in the country?" Her voice lifted interrogatively.

"I'm city-bred, I'm afraid," Leonora admitted. "This is all new and strange to me. Before this, the closest I've been to wildlife was hearing the dawn chorus when the birds woke up in Grammercy Park."

"Poor you," Clio sympathized. "And now you have owls hooting in the night, foxes barking, crickets, cows, sheep and other assorted animals and insects all making their own weird noises."

"And some of them can sound awfully weird in the middle of the night. For instance . . ." Leonora paused, then plunged on. "What kind of animal makes a noise like footsteps on a gravel path?"

"Footsteps on a gravel path?" Clio frowned and appeared to be considering the question seriously. "You've got me. Are you sure they *weren't* footsteps?"

"I hope they weren't." Leonora laughed nervously. "They were right outside my window."

"I shouldn't let that bother you." But Clio was still frowning. "It was probably just James on one of his nocturnal strolls. He has insomnia quite badly and he's always out prowling around in the small hours. It would never have occurred to him that you might be awake and that he might be frightening you."

"I wasn't frightened exactly," Leonora said. "Just uneasy. Now that I know what—and who—it is, I shan't worry about it any more."

"I'll have a quiet word with James."

"No, please! Don't bother him about it. I'd feel silly. It's all right, now that I know."

"Perhaps it would be better if I didn't," Clio agreed, a trifle too quickly. "Poor James, he has his problems." She laughed uneasily. "Of course, I suppose we could all say that."

"I suppose we could," Leonora said distantly. If that was a veiled invitation to confide her own troubles, she was not about to accept it.

"Here we are." Clio swerved around a corner and a town was suddenly revealed at the bottom of the hill. "With luck, we'll find a parking place near Anselm's, then we can have that coffee."

"Actually—" Leonora reverted to the subject over coffee and delicious little cream cakes—"I halfway thought that the footsteps might belong to someone else. James never occurred to me, but when I looked out of the window I could see a light burning in one of the upstairs rooms over the front door of the manor house."

"Oh, that would be Eddie's home office," Clio said. "He'd never be strolling around—he's lost to the world when he gets entrenched up there. Rather, he's lost to *us* and wide open to the rest of the world. That's where he keeps his computer and all its equipment. He's in touch with stock markets all over the world up there. You'll get the guided tour sooner or later and he'll show you his computer and his bank of clocks giving the time in New York and Tokyo and Sydney and Hong Kong—and Timbuctoo, for all I know. I just smile and stop listening, but you needn't worry about Eddie. He doesn't go strolling around. Once he's up there, he forgets this place exists. He stays up there most of the night sometimes and only comes down to rush off to the City. It drives poor Bunty frantic.''

''Mmm-hmm...'' It was hard to imagine Bunty frantic; it was much easier to visualize her driving everyone else frantic. Perhaps Eddie's home office was his only escape from her.

''Of course,'' Clio went on, ''we understand that sometimes he *has* to keep on top of the international situation. When the stock markets started crashing all over the world, for instance, he didn't dare even spare the time to travel to the City. He shut himself up in his tower and didn't even come down for meals. Bunty brought them up to him herself and half the time he wouldn't open the door to her, he was so involved. And she had to come over to my place to make any telephone calls because he kept the line tied up solidly for two weeks. I wouldn't like to have had their telephone bill!''

''It was a very difficult time everywhere.'' Paul had lost a lot of money on the New York Stock Exchange at that time. It had not helped his temper nor sweetened his disposition.

''Difficult! I've never seen Eddie looking so haggard—the few glimpses I caught of him. Truthfully, I was almost afraid to go out in the morning. I was half afraid I'd find his body sprawled on the path beneath his window.''

''They didn't seem to hurl themselves out of windows this time around,'' Leonora said. ''Perhaps everyone learned that much of a lesson from the 1929 Crash: it doesn't do them any good and only makes things worse for their widows and orphans."

"That's very true." Clio gave Leonora a guilty sideways glance and changed the subject. "Don't you think this view is beautiful?"

"Beautiful. We seem so remote from all that sort of thing here." Belatedly, Leonora remembered that she was masquerading as a widow and realized that Clio was afraid that her reference to death might have been tactless.

"We are, really," Clio said eagerly. "Most of us."

Leonora sipped her coffee and looked down at the town spread out below. A peaceful symphony of grey stone buildings and green squares, it sprawled comfortably across the valley, bisected by a narrow river gleaming in the sunlight and bordered by the hills surrounding it.

"Highmarsh just misses being a Cathedral city." Clio followed her gaze. "The church is old enough, but it isn't grand enough."

"It's very beautiful, though."

"Thank heavens it escaped the worst excesses of the Sixties. The Town Council refused planning permission to the developers who wanted to tear down the center of town and rebuild it in 'modern' style. I understand Lady Cosgreave's late husband led the fight, so the people hereabouts have quite a bit to thank the family for. Not that I expect they do."

"It would make a good picture," Leonora mused aloud. "Painted from this angle, looking down on the scene . . ."

"What a good idea!" Clio was instantly enthusiastic. "I'm sure we could get you permission. You could set up your easel in a corner, you wouldn't take up much room." She was on her feet. "I'll speak to the Manager. I'm sure he'll allow it. I'm sure he'll be delighted."

"No, please. I couldn't do it for ages. I have to finish the canvases I have blocked out for the exhibition before I can think of doing any new work."

"Oh." Clio sank back into her chair, crestfallen. "I'm sorry. I just thought . . . as long as we're right here . . ."

"Why don't we just shop today?" Leonora suggested. "That's what we came to do."

"That's right!" Clio brightened again. "So we did! Let's start!" She caught up the bill and hurried towards the cashier, Leonora trailing in her wake, protesting that *she* had intended to pay for coffee.

"No, no," Clio insisted. "It's *my* treat—and you have no idea what a treat it is for me to have someone to go shopping with."

They were browsing in the Chinaware Department when a tall, thin man in a dark suit with a rosebud in his buttonhole suddenly appeared beside them, frowning.

"Why, here he is now!" Clio exclaimed delightedly. "Mr. Maynard, the Manager of Anselm's. We were just talking about you, Mr. Maynard." She beamed up into his less-than-ecstatic face. "This is my new neighbor, Leonora Rice, the famous American artist. She was so admiring the view from the roof terrace just now. I promised her I'd speak to you about giving her permission to set up her easel and do a painting of it."

"Indeed?" The cold face thawed slightly, but the eyes remained hard as he sketched a bow towards Leonora, who tried not to cringe. It was precisely the sort of introduction she most hated—and it evidently hadn't cut a great deal of ice with Mr. Maynard, either.

"You will allow her to, won't you, Mr. Maynard?" Clio pressed winsomely. "I'm sure it would be marvelous publicity for Anselm's and the customers would enjoy having a famous artist in their midst and being able to watch her work and see how the painting was coming along each day."

"Well . . ." Mr. Maynard looked at Clio thoughtfully. "She wouldn't take up much room, would she? Just she alone? By herself?"

No one had asked Leonora how she might feel about being part of the floor show. For a moment she still cherished the hope that permission might be refused.

"Hardly any room at all," Clio assured him. "She'd just tuck herself away with her easel and palette in a quiet corner and you'd hardly notice she was there . . . just her."

"Really," Leonora protested, "this isn't necessary. I wouldn't want to be any trouble——"

"No, no——" Mr. Maynard was apparently warming to the idea. "We can find you a quiet corner quite easily. One where people can't come and look over your shoulder."

"That would be kind." Leonora smiled gratefully. Mr. Maynard had more sensitivity than Clio. "But I shan't be able to take up your generous offer for some while yet. I have several other paintings to finish first."

"Whenever you wish." Mr. Maynard bowed again. "Just let me know. *You* will always be welcome here."

Leonora blinked. There had been a faint, deadly emphasis on that *you*. She glanced at Clio, who was blandly toying with her handbag.

More strangely, despite the note of farewell in his last remark, Mr. Maynard showed no sign of departing. He hovered silently, the conversation ended but the participants unable to break away.

"Heavens, look at the time!" It was Clio who broke the impasse. "I must run and feed my parking meter. You needn't hurry, Leonora, I can meet you back at the car later."

"No, I'll come along." Leonora discovered that she would be glad to get away. There was something vaguely sinister about Mr. Maynard's hovering presence.

He bowed again and stood watching them as they turned and left, trying not to look as though they were rushing away.

"He's a very nice man, really," Clio said apologetically as they emerged from the revolving door at the front of

Anselm's. "There's just . . . something about it. Sometimes he makes me very nervous."

"I know what you mean," Leonora said. "I felt it, too."

"Did you? I'm so glad. Tom keeps telling me it's just my imagination. He says I'm always imagining that people are behaving oddly, when they're acting quite naturally. Sometimes it makes me wonder . . ." She let the thought trail off into a cloud of self-doubt.

"Well, you weren't wrong this time," Leonora said with renewed sympathy. Again, she equated the absent Tom with Paul in her mind. It would be interesting to meet him—when he returned.

"Anyway—" Clio unlocked the car—"let's go to the supermarket next. It's the best place to pick up those light-bulbs you wanted. And you said you needed supplies, as well."

CHAPTER 7

For the rest of the week, Leonora kept to her resolution to stay in the cottage and work, her determination strengthened by the fact that the work was going so well.

Evidently Clio had spread the word that she was not to be disturbed, for the neighbours were very forbearing. Not even Annabel Hinchby-Smythe imposed upon the peace of her days and there were no more footsteps in the night. Or, if there were, she didn't hear them, perhaps because she no longer lingered downstairs long enough to fall asleep. Now that she had proper lighting, she could return to her studio after dinner and continue working up there.

It was too good to last and of course it didn't.

The first high-powered motors began roaring up the drive at about three-thirty on Friday afternoon. At one point, she looked out of the window, but was able to identify the automobiles only as fast and racy sports models.

The later arrivals were still powerful, but more sedate, doubtless their owners were the same, but most of them were hidden behind smoked-glass windows. Sleek, opulent and expensive, the limousines were the sort Paul would have cheerfully killed to acquire.

It looked as though it were going to be an extremely social weekend up at the manor house. With sudden unease, Leonora tried to recall just what Annabel had been saying earlier in the week . . . something about all hands to the pump when Bunty entertained . . .

The thought trailed off and she returned to work. It was twilight before she became aware of the outside world again and then it was borne in on her abruptly.

A faint scent of smoke drifted through the air, alerting her to possible danger. She dropped her brush in the jar without even wiping it and hurried to the top of the stairs. The smell was stronger there, coming from somewhere downstairs. Had she forgotten to turn off the cooker?

Half way down the stairs, the smell became identifiable as cigarette smoke. Someone was in the house, smoking. Bunty again? Did Bunty smoke?

Leonora continued her descent, making rather more noise than necessary. In the hallway below, a tall figure emerged from the living-room and squinted up at her.

"Hey, you're looking great," he said. "You've lost some weight and—oh, my God!"

Leonora paused a few steps above him and looked down on his embarrassment. It was acute.

"I'm sorry, lady. I'm so sorry. I was just—I mean, I was—"

"If you're looking for someone," Leonora said, "I'm afraid you have the wrong house."

"I'll say I have! This is terrible. I can't apologize enough. I didn't know anyone was living here. I mean—" He broke off, in more confusion than before.

Leonora smiled and refrained from asking him why he had just greeted someone he obviously expected to see if he thought the house was unoccupied. Possibly he was a leftover friend of the Ordways who had forgotten they had gone back to Canada.

"I thought I'd just slip in for a minute and sneak a cigarette before I checked in at the Hall." He had apparently decided on the most face-saving story now. "Ever since Eddie—you know Eddie?" He waited for her nod.

"Ever since Eddie gave up smoking, he's been hell-on-wheels about other people smoking. I couldn't stand another goddam sanctimonious lecture from him—not to start off the weekend."

"I see." Leonora kept smiling. It was obviously unnerving him more than anything else she could have done.

"Yeah, well—" He looked around helplessly, holding the offending cigarette at arm's length, trying to dissociate himself from it. "I'm very sorry to have disturbed you like this. I—I'll be getting along now."

"Goodbye," Leonora said sweetly. Most definitely, she was going to see about having that lock changed first thing on Monday morning. It was quite obvious that Bunty and the cleaning woman were not the only ones with a key to the cottage. It seemed that the Ordways had been very friendly people. Too friendly, perhaps. She wondered how many more keys were floating around.

"Yeah, well—" Her unexpected visitor had opened the front door with every appearance of relief at getting away so easily. "I'll just apologize again and—" He stared at her pleadingly.

For the first time Leonora realized what the phrase "an agony of embarrassment" meant. The man was almost twisting himself into knots.

"Look—" he blurted out. "This will probably sound awful but—I mean, we'll probably be meeting socially—me staying up at Cosgreave Hall and you living so near—"

"We probably will," Leonora admitted.

"Well, look—you don't have to tell anybody about this, do you? I mean, I feel enough of a fool without everybody knowing about it and snickering at me—"

"We'll meet as strangers," Leonora said. "In fact, we are."

"That's great. Thanks a lot." He was out the door before

she could say anything else, shutting it swiftly behind him as though afraid she might have second thoughts.

She listened to his retreating footsteps as he stepped off the path and cut across the gravel. They did not sound the same as those other footsteps, but they brought a disquieting thought. Did that other person also have a key to the cottage? She was beginning to feel very vulnerable.

Definitely the locksmith on Monday morning. She wouldn't even mention it to Bunty. She'd get the new locks first and turn the keys over to Bunty when she left. And only then.

Meanwhile, she had nothing further to fear from her late visitor; he would be in no hurry to see her again. Fortunately, he had not recognized her as a fellow-American. Of course, she hadn't said much and he had been so busy trying to explain himself that he would not have noticed even if her accent had been much stronger than it actually was.

He must also be quite a close friend—or associate—of Eddie's, since he seemed to be a regular at the weekend house-parties and certainly knew his way around the enclave. Rather too well. He was anxious not to have his trespassing disclosed, so perhaps he was not quite such a close friend, after all. Either that, or Eddie was more paranoiac about smoking than one might suspect.

Leonora frowned. She was sure that some people had been smoking at the Sunday morning drinks session, but she could not quite recall who. Eddie had not seemed to mind then.

A knocking at the back door brought her back to the present. She hurried to open the door. Had her strange visitor had afterthoughts and returned?

"Hope you don't mind my dropping in like this." Annabel stood there. "But I just saw Phil Mottram leaving and thought that you must be available for socializing again."

"Oh, er, come in." But Annabel was already across the threshold and heading for the living-room. "I've been meaning to return your plate and pitcher but . . ."

"You've been busy. I know. There's no rush. I have others." Annabel dropped on to the sofa, obviously ready for a long visit.

"Would you like a cup of tea?" As Annabel's face registered controlled disgust, Leonora added hastily, "Or a martini?"

"A martini would be very nice." Annabel's face cleared. "I suppose Phil came down to bring you your summons."

"Summons?" Leonora was lost but didn't like to admit it. She hadn't even known the man's name, but she was still conscious of her promise to him. It was too bad Annabel had seen him at the cottage. Clearly Annabel knew him and thought she knew why he had visited the cottage. "What summons?"

"I see." Annabel nodded as though a private suspicion had just been confirmed. "Never mind, it will come."

"I'll just make the martinis—" Leonora fled kitchenwards, feeling that a pitcher of martinis might be a necessary adjunct to any conversation with Annabel. "I won't be a minute."

"Take your time," Annabel said, picking up a magazine. "I'm in no hurry."

That was just what Leonora feared. She splashed gin into glasses, added a drop of bitters and far more vermouth, she was sure, than Annabel would like. Recklessly, she added ice cubes, positive that Annabel would hate them, but she didn't like her own martinis too strong and it would have been rather pointed to serve two different strengths.

When she returned with the tray of drinks and nibbles, Annabel was no longer on the sofa but prowling the room, the magazine discarded on the coffee table.

"Ah—" Annabel turned away from her inspection of the ornaments on the mantelpiece with obvious dissatisfaction which did not improve as she looked at the lumps of ice floating in the drinks. "I thought you Americans always had your drinks—what's the expression?—straight up."

"Not all of us," Leonora said demurely. "You can, if you like, though. Next round."

"I can't stand seeing good spirits drowned!" Annabel fished out the ice cubes and dropped them in the ashtray on top of the ashes. "Oh, I didn't know you smoked."

"Er, occasionally." Leonora felt that she was getting in too deep. That ridiculous man—Phil Mottram—had left her with too many things to explain and he ought to have known better. If he was a regular visitor, he surely must have known that there would be eyes watching whatever he did. He must be an idiot to think he could slip into the cottage unnoticed.

"Mmm . . ." Annabel sank half her drink in one gulp. "Always said this was an interesting place to live."

"It certainly seems to be a busy place this weekend."

"Never a dull moment." Annabel met her eyes meaningfully. "As I'm sure you're discovering."

"I *did* expect it to be a bit quieter down here—" Another high-powered car roared towards the drive, drowning the rest of her words.

"If you ask me," Annabel said darkly, "they're getting up a Concert Party."

She sounded so disapproving that Leonora could only assume that she must be a music-hater.

A sudden squeal of brakes and a crash outside sent them both hurtling towards the window.

"What is it? What happened?"

"Can you see anything?" Annabel clawed at the curtains.

"Not much, it's too dark." Leonora could just discern the black shape of a sports car crunched up against the stone gatepost.

"Misjudged the turn, I'd say." Annabel let the curtain drop back and headed for the front door. "Let's see if they need help."

A shaken young woman was alone in the car, her head resting on the steering-wheel. She had turned the engine off and there appeared to be no imminent danger of fire or explosion.

"Are you all right?" Annabel rapped on the side window. "Are you all right in there?"

Slowly the girl pushed herself away from the steering-wheel, rubbed her forehead and winced, then fumbled for the door handle.

"That's right." Annabel swung open the door. "Get out and take a few deep breaths. Get some air into you. Are you hurt or just shocked?"

"Just shocked, I think." As advised, the girl breathed deeply. "I'm sorry. Just as I turned . . . a cat . . . or a small dog . . . ran in front of me. I swerved to avoid it and—"

"No dogs or cats here," Annabel said. "No pets at all. It must have been a fox. Plenty of them around here."

"It was . . . something . . ." Dazedly, the girl shook her head, then seemed to regret the action. Her hands rose to clutch at her forehead, stopping the movement.

"You'd better come into the house." Annabel had taken command of the situation. "You need to lie down and rest."

"No. No, thank you. I'll be all right in a moment." Several deep breaths—more like gasps—and she continued, "Sorry to be such a nuisance."

"Nonsense! Just come inside." Annabel had her by the arm and was urging her along, less from concern than from curiosity, Leonora suspected.

"No, really—" The girl balked and it was too late. The front door of Cosgreave Hall had opened and people were streaming down the driveway. "I'll be all right!"

"Tessa! It's Tessa Andrews!" someone called. "Tessa, what happened?"

"Oh, bad luck!" They were surrounding her now, pushing Annabel into the background. "Is the car all right?"

"Just scratched, I think."

"Bit worse than that, I'm afraid, old girl," one of the group inspecting the damage called out. "You're going to need a new bumper. It's going to set you back a fair bit. Or your insurance company."

"Oh damn!" she said. "There goes my no-claims bonus."

"Next time, hit the animal," someone else advised callously. "It will work out cheaper."

"One-two-and threeee. One-two-and-threeee—" Some of the men had begun rocking the car free of the post. "Easy now—" There was a grinding noise and a tinkle of glass as the headlight fell out of its frame.

"Try the motor . . . will it start?" One of the men got into the car and turned the ignition key. After a preliminary demur, the motor grumbled into life.

"It will do," the driver decided. "Let's get it up to the garage. Eddie can get a mechanic round in the morning. Come on, Tessa, want a lift?"

"Phil—?" Tessa lifted her head to look around at the dark figures surrounding her. "Is Phil here?"

"Sorry," an anonymous voice answered. "Phil stayed up at the house. Didn't think it sounded serious."

In the darkness, someone snickered.

"Do you want to get back in the car?" Eddie, his arm supporting Tessa, asked solicitously.

"No . . . no. I'd rather walk."

"Okay, take it easy. Lean on me. Slowly, now." Eddie led her up the driveway in the wake of the laboring car and its cheering entourage.

"That's strange." Shunted firmly to the sideline with Annabel, Leonora looked after the crowd of noisy strangers, as they straggled up the driveway. "I didn't see Bunty there, did you?"

"Knowing Bunty," Annabel said caustically, "I'd bet that she's improving the shining hour. Or perhaps she's rolling bandages, boiling soup and filling the brandy casks of the St. Bernards."

"Oh!" Leonora was startled into tactlessness. "You don't really like Bunty, do you?"

"Nonsense!" Annabel said. "Haven't you ever heard

Dinah on the subject? To know Bunty is to—'' She broke off sharply.

"Why are we standing here gossiping?" she demanded. "Don't know about you, but I could use another drink. Can't fly on one wing! *You* are being derelict in your hostess duties.''

"Oh, I'm sorry. I didn't mean—'' Leonora was unsure how or why she had been put so firmly in the wrong. "Do come back to the house and I'll—''

"Oh no you won't,'' Annabel said firmly. "*I* will mix the next batch of drinks.''

CHAPTER 8

Leonora's dreams that night were troubled, but she had grown to expect that. Vague shadowy figures lurking just beyond the edges of her consciousness; footsteps crunched on gravel paths; and—a new addition—high-powered motor-cars revved up and roared up and down the driveway past the front of the cottage. Even at the back of the cottage, phantoms came and went, accompanied by the barking of foxes and hooting of owls.

She awoke more exhausted than she had been when she retired. She lay blinking at the still unfamiliar ceiling, wondering whether it might, after all, be better to give up this idea of country peace and move back to the city where she could identify her sources of unease and perhaps do something about them.

It was too long—far too long—before she realized that she was wasting precious minutes of bright daylight by lying here and thinking about things that were essentially none of her business. Her business was to paint.

She got up and went straight to her studio, not even bothering to get dressed. Her dressing-gown was warm enough. She was expecting no visitors. Upon Annabel's departure last night, she had carefully bolted every door and locked every window. Anyone who gained entrance now would be admitting possession of unlawful keys and, somehow, she did not think anyone would be willing to admit that.

The painting went well for about an hour, then she decided to break for a meal. If she told herself it was brunch, she wouldn't feel she had missed breakfast, simply combined the two meals. And, she told herself sternly, it was high time she got dressed. Although the cottage purported to be centrally heated, it had not the warmth she was accustomed to in the States. Perhaps the pervading dampness of the climate had something to do with it.

She dressed and put the kettle on, then opened the back door to see if it was really as mild and pleasant outside as it looked. It was, and she inhaled deeply of the soft country air. A lovely day, perhaps too lovely to spend it all indoors. In the distance, Molly waved a pair of secateurs at her from the flowerbed where she was busily helping herself to a bouquet of autumn blooms.

Leonora waved back and turned to go into the house before Molly took it for an invitation to come down and visit. Out of the corner of her eye, she caught a glimpse of something in the bushes beside the gravel path curving up to the manor house.

She hesitated. Even in the short time she had been living here, she had noticed how beautifully the grounds were kept. It was most unusual to see any litter. Perhaps it was something that had fallen off the car after the accident last night, although it did not seem to be either metal or glass.

She had hesitated too long. Molly began sauntering towards her, beaming and sure of her welcome. She was trapped. Oh well . . .

"Kettle's boiling," she said, as Molly came within earshot. "How about a cup of coffee?"

"Wonderful." Molly thrust the armload of flowers at her as they went inside. "Have some flowers. I'll cut some more for Bunty, she won't begrudge you these. There are plenty more."

"Thank you, they're lovely." Leonora accepted them, albeit with reservations about Bunty's attitude. If she were genuinely unlikely to begrudge them, it would not have been necessary to mention it. "I was just thinking how nice everything looked and how well-kept the grounds were."

"Yes," Molly said drily. "We can all take a bow for that."

"That's right," Leonora remembered. "You all pitch in to help, don't you?"

"Giles is especially good at it," Molly said. "It's that Army background. You know: If it moves, salute it; if it doesn't move, pick it up; if you can't pick it up, paint it."

Leonora laughed with her. "I suppose I ought to begin doing my part, now that I'm living here. I saw a bit of rubbish under the big bush just now, perhaps I ought to go and pick it up."

"It must have blown in during the night," Molly said. "Giles policed the grounds quite thoroughly yesterday afternoon. Because of the houseparty, you know. We like to have everything looking nice for Eddie's posh City friends."

"I met some of them yesterday." Leonora poured the coffee. "Well, not quite *met*. I saw them after that girl ran into the gatepost. In fact, I thought the bit under the bush might be from her car."

"Oh dear—" Molly had been comfortably settled at the table, now she pushed back her chair. "I ought to go and retrieve it, then. It might be something vital. I don't know much about cars, but I do know that anything missing from one is automatically its most important part. Where did you say it was?"

"Over there." Leonora walked to the door with her and indicated the spot. Molly moved towards it and she followed.

"I don't see—Oh!" Abruptly, Molly stopped dead, staring down at something protruding from beneath the bush.

"It's a shoe." Leonora thought back, but could not recall anyone limping around without a shoe last night. if there had been, some of the others would have noticed it and probably made jokes about it.

"It's more than that, I'm afraid," Molly said.

"Oh!" Leonora looked closely and saw that it was not an empty shoe. "Is it—? Is it a tramp sleeping off—?" She faltered and stopped. It was a well-made shoe in good repair with a small triangular craftsman's mark on the sole. Not a tramp's shoe, at all. And it was very still. It had not moved since she had first noticed it, earlier that morning. Even voices discussing it close by were not disturbing its owner.

"Is he . . . sick?" Anything worse was unthinkable. Leonora pushed back the fear curling through her consciousness.

"I don't know." Molly dropped to her hands and knees. "I'll find out."

"Be careful."

"It's all right . . ." Molly's voice was muffled as she crawled under the bush. "I was a nurse before I met Giles."

"Can I do anything?" Leonora crouched, trying to see what was happening, but the bush was too thick and forbidding. There was no room for anyone else in the small clearing under those drooping leafy branches. "I feel so useless."

"Oh no!" Molly gasped and then there was silence.

"What is it?" Leonora called anxiously. "What's wrong?" Deep down, something told her that she really did not want to know.

"Just a moment—" There was a rustling sound, then another silence.

"No, it's all right." Molly announced. "It's so dark under here. For a moment I thought he was . . . someone else."

"He's all right." Leonora felt weak with relief.

"I didn't say that." Molly's voice was faint and troubled. "Just stand by—we may have a first-class emergency on our hands."

"He *is* sick! I'll go and call for an ambulance." That was something she could do.

"Hold hard!" Molly's voice was sharp. "I'm coming out." There was an upheaval among the branches and Molly backed out, looking as though she had been dragged through a hedge backwards—as, indeed, she almost had. Her face was grim as she rose to her feet, brushing off twigs and dead leaves.

"What is it? What's the matter with him?"

"Matter enough, he's dead." Molly finished adjusting her dress and began adjusting the branches. "Let's get back to your place."

"But we can't just leave him there!"

"Believe me—" Molly met Leonora's protesting eyes— "if there was anything I could do for him, I would. There isn't—and we've got to think of the living."

"But what happened? How did he die—could you tell? And why was he under the bush?" Leonora shuddered. Had he crawled under it like a sick animal, to hide and die there?

"I don't know." Molly briskly led the way back to the cottage, as though there were thoughts she wanted to outdistance. "We'll have to tell Eddie."

"Yes, but shouldn't we call an ambulance just the same?" Leonora hurried to keep up with Molly's lengthening stride. "Or the police?"

"First," Molly said, "we must talk to Eddie."

"But don't your police get upset if you don't notify them right away? I know ours would."

"Time enough." Molly cast a grim glance backwards. "There's no reason why they shouldn't know they weren't informed immediately."

"But . . ." Leonora also glanced backward, following Molly's gaze. The bush now looked undisturbed and somehow bushier. Was it just a coincidence that Molly had rearranged the branches so that they now hid the tell-tale foot?

* * *

"As I see it," Eddie said slowly, "it's too bad about Horton, but the last thing any of us wants at this moment in time is to be caught up in the middle of a police investigation."

There were murmurs of agreement and Leonora was conscious of uneasy surreptitious glances in her direction. She was not one of them; they could not be sure of her reaction. She knew that she would not even have been included in the conference if it were not for the fact that she had discovered the body.

"Was that his name?" Leonora asked. "Horton? You knew him?"

"It took me a moment to recognize him—" Molly laughed shakily and turned to Bunty. "I didn't know you'd finally persuaded Eddie to part with that ghastly 'Country Gentlemen' suit of his."

"He did it without telling me." Bunty gave Eddie a *You'll hear more about this later* look. "He knew I'd be furious at his giving it to Horton. The man has made a constant nuisance of himself and Eddie shouldn't be encouraging him by giving him anything more. He's had enough—too much!"

"I gave it to him before all the trouble started. He's had it for ages." Eddie defended himself, then launched an attack of his own. "You didn't even notice it was gone." He brooded further. "Nobody noticed.

"But who was Horton?" Leonora persisted.

"He used to be the gardener here," Molly said reluctantly, admitting her right to be told something. "Before he was let go."

"We didn't need him any more." Eddie was still defensive. "Not after we sold off the river acreage. Besides, he was tying up valuable property, freeloading off of us."

"That's a bit hard," Giles protested. "The gardener has always had a tied cottage. It's considered part of his wages."

"They were always too high! *And*—" Bunty glared at her husband—"he got too many perks."

"Look, just cool it, will you?" Eddie snapped. Leonora suspected that he wished he had left Bunty at home, but that probably wasn't so easy to do.

Molly's second telephone call had been to Giles and he had arrived immediately behind Bunty and Eddie and taken up his place by Molly's side. Leonora suspected that Molly had telephoned everyone because she had not dared leave Leonora unattended for fear of what she might do.

So far, no one had telephoned the police.

"We wanted the cottage to let out," Eddie said stubbornly. "Horton had no right to it any longer. His right ended when his job ended. He was deliberately making a nuisance of himself."

"Oh, quite," Giles said hastily. "Just the same—" He winced. "The eviction was rather nasty. I mean, calling in the bailiffs—that was going a bit far."

"We were within *our* rights." Eddie glared at him, still on the defensive.

In her corner, Bunty had lit a cigarette and was amusing herself by blowing smoke rings—almost a lost art in these anti-smoking times. She did not appear to be listening to the argument at all.

"Do you mean this cottage used to belong to that man?" Leonora asked uneasily.

"Of course not," Eddie said. "The cottage always belonged to the Cosgreave Hall Estate. He just had the use of it—for as long as he worked for us. Unfortunately, he took it badly when we had to turn him out. He believed he was still entitled to it and used to come back and prowl around. I think he thought he'd get the cottage back if the tenants left. We had to chase him away several times."

"It was such a bore," Bunty said. "And the Ordways *did* leave suddenly. I'm sure it was because Horton made such a nuisance of himself."

"There was someone prowling around here a few nights

ago," Leonora said. "I heard footsteps on the gravel, but couldn't see anyone when I looked out."

"There you are!" Bunty said. "Up to his old tricks again! I told you, Eddie, we should do something about him."

"Actually," Molly said, "it seems as though someone has."

There was an awkward pause. Then Bunty made a noise that was more of a nervous bray than a laugh and blew another smoke ring. If the performance was supposed to demonstrate nonchalance, it was a failure.

"How *did* Horton die?" Giles asked.

"Head injuries," Molly said. "Of course, one can never be sure without an autopsy but, from the look of him . . ."

"He was always quarrelsome," Eddie said. "Sounds as though he got into a fight at the pub and got the worst of it. Then he forgot where he belonged and came back here to die."

"That would be just like him," Bunty agreed. "Still making a nuisance of himself—alive or dead."

She and Eddie nodded emphatically at each other. They seemed to have settled the matter to their own satisfaction—if no one else's.

"The point is—" Giles called them to order—"what are we to do about it?"

There was another awkward silence. Everyone looked at each other and then at Leonora. It was obvious that they wished she would go home and leave them to come to a decision by themselves.

Unfortunately for them, she *was* home—or what passed for it these days. She had paid a quarter's rent in advance and they could not ask her to leave the room in her own house. Bunty looked as though she might be considering it, however.

"We can't just leave him there," Leonora said, suspecting that was just what they would like to do. She emphasized the "we" slightly, making it clear that she had included herself in the decision-making.

"Of course not!" Molly was the only one who looked shocked at the idea; the others just looked regretful.

"Pity he had to die here, of all places," Giles said. "Makes it a bit awkward, what?"

"I know!" Bunty said. "Why don't we take him back to the pub? That's where it must have happened—and it isn't fair that we should be dragged into it. The men can carry him back and leave him where the pubkeeper can find him." She looked around and smiled brightly. "After dark, of course."

"I don't see how you can be so sure he got his injuries in a pub brawl," Leonora protested. "Aren't you forgetting something?"

"That's the only way it could have happened." Bunty looked at her coldly.

"What are you suggesting?" Giles asked.

"There was an automobile accident right outside here last night," Leonora reminded them. "The driver claimed she swerved to avoid a small animal. Perhaps she did—but she might have avoided the animal and hit the man. He could have been knocked into the bushes and—"

"Jesus!" Eddie stared at her, aghast. "You can't involve Tessa Andrews in this!"

"I'm not saying she knew that she had done it. If she was concentrating on missing the animal, and the man was standing on the side of the road as she swerved—it would have been an accident and she might not have realized it happened."

"Not even if it was an accident!" Eddie had gone pale. "Do you know who she is?" He went a shade paler. "Do you know who her father is?"

"Just the same, old man," Giles said, "it's a distinct possibility. If Horton had been knocked unconscious instantly—" He looked to Molly inquiringly.

"He would have been," she confirmed. "And then there was so much noise and commotion when everyone came running to see what had happened—"

"No one would have heard Horton, even if he'd regained consciousness enough to moan," Giles concluded for her. "Everyone was too concerned with Tessa to think of looking around to see if anyone else might have been injured."

"I don't believe it!" Eddie said. "Tessa couldn't have hit someone without noticing it. I mean, I suppose she could have, but—"

"If she had known it," Bunty said thoughtfully, "that doesn't necessarily mean she'd have mentioned it. I got the impression that she'd had a drink or three before she left Town. If that little contretemps with the gatepost on private land had turned into something that meant the police would arrive with their little breathalyzers . . . she'd have lost more than her no-claims bonus."

"Bunty!" Eddie looked at her as though she were a traitor. "Honey, don't even think of such a thing!"

The doorbell shrilled into the sudden silence, making them all jump.

"Who's there?" Eddie demanded accusingly of Leonora.

"I don't know," she said. "I'm not expecting anyone."

Molly tiptoed to the window as the doorbell pealed again.

"Oh God!" she reported. "It's Annabel! Isn't that all we need just now?"

CHAPTER 9

"Don't let her in!" Bunty said instantly. "Don't answer the door and she'll go away." The others looked highly sceptical.

"It won't work," Leonora said. "She knows I'm here."

"She knows we're all here," Molly said resignedly.

The doorbell rang again.

"I really must . . ." Leonora moved towards the hall.

"Oh, I suppose so!" Bunty threw herself back in her chair and pouted. "If you don't, she'll think there's something wrong."

"Don't tell her anything," Eddie said urgently. "We'll talk about this again later."

It was all most unsatisfactory, but they were right about one thing: if Annabel got wind of the situation, it would only make things worse.

Her hand on the doorknob, Leonora paused. What was she thinking? The police were going to have to be called, so what difference did it make whether Annabel knew or not? She realized that the urgency of the others had been drawing her into a spiral of conspiracy. Perhaps it was just as well that Annabel had shown up just now; she needed another outsider, without ulterior motives, to help her keep her balance.

Leonora smoothed her frown into a passable resemblance to a welcoming smile and opened the door as the doorbell shrilled again.

"There you are!" Annabel greeted her. "I'd begun to think you were at the top of the house and had fallen downstairs rushing to answer the bell."

"Nothing so dramatic," Leonora said drily. The truth was more so, rather than less. "Do come in."

"Thought you might like to drop over for a drink—" Annabel preceded her into the living-room and stopped stagily just inside the door.

"Hello, Annabel," the others chorused resignedly.

"Oh, I'm sorry—" Annabel said. "I didn't realize you were having a party." Her sharp gaze swept the room, noting the absence of any signs of conviviality.

"We were just leaving," Bunty said, rising from her chair. "We just stopped by for a moment to invite Leonora for drinks and a buffet luncheon tomorrow. In fact, we were on our way to you next. You will come, won't you?"

"Thank you." Annabel's gaze took the merest flick towards the telephone, making it obvious that such invitations were not usually conveyed in person. "I'd be delighted."

"Wonderful! We'll see you all tomorrow, then. Twelve-thirtyish." Bunty's hand closed over Leonora's forearm in a grip of steel, drawing her to the front door with her departing guests.

Leonora glanced back over her shoulder in time to see Annabel turn expectantly to Molly and Giles, who had been left to provide their own explanation for their presence.

"Don't say anything to her." Bunty's urgent whisper was half way between a command and a plea. "And don't *do* anything! I'll get back to you later about this."

"Please—" Eddie weighed in. "You don't know how important it is that nothing be allowed to ruin this weekend. We'll tackle the situation first thing Monday morning. What difference can a few hours make?"

"But . . ." Leonora told herself she should have foreseen this. Already, Eddie's "few hours" were stretching out into double figures. Monday morning? What difference? It would give their precious Tessa Andrews time to get back to London, to her own garage, to have that crumpled bumper replaced and all trace of damage removed. Of course there was no proof that the girl had been responsible for the death—but there never would be if she got her car repaired before the police examined it.

"At least, don't do anything until we've had a chance to talk to you again," Bunty pleaded. "Mummy's coming down tonight. She'll know what to do. She's a friend of the Chief Constable."

"Well . . ." Leonora hesitated and was lost.

"Promise!" Bunty insisted.

"Great!" Eddie took the promise as already given and wrung her hand. "You won't regret this."

As the door closed behind them, Leonora was regretting it already. She regretted it even more after Molly and Giles had taken their hasty leave and departed.

"All right." Annabel turned on her. "What are they up to?"

"Up to?" she echoed faintly.

"Don't try to tell me they're not! I know them of old. I've seen that expression on their faces before."

"Really?" Leonora fervently hoped not. How many dead bodies could they have had in their bushes?

"You haven't signed anything, have you?" Annabel's nose twitched suspiciously.

"Of course not."

"Well, don't! I don't know what your financial situation is—?"

"I'm managing to keep my head above water."

"Good!" Annabel had clearly hoped for more information than that. "Keep it that way. Don't get caught up in any of their get-rich-quick schemes. The only one who ever seems to get rich out of them is Eddie."

"Honestly, they've never even suggested such a thing." But it cast an interesting new light on Bunty and Eddie.

"Early days yet. Just make sure they're not softening you up for the kill. Eddie thinks he's cut out to be everyone's financial adviser—for a hefty fee, of course. I keep telling him that all my funds are tied up by Trustees. Barely give me enough allowance to keep me in gin. I'd never let him get his hands on any of my money."

"Not having any in the first place, I shan't have to worry about that."

"Just watch yourself. Whenever those two give one of their big weekend parties, it's time to keep clear and hang on to your wool—because someone's going to get fleeced!"

"It wouldn't be worth their while to waste any time on me." Leonora was intrigued.

"Then they must be gunning for someone else." Annabel's eyes narrowed as she considered the possibilities. "Mmm . . . I've noticed that Phil Mottram is here again. Practically taking up residence. Sixth houseparty in a row he's attended. *And* he's richer than Croesus. Must be something going on there."

Leonora made a noncommittal sound. Her own thoughts flew to Tessa Andrews. Eddie had been very concerned that nothing should upset her—or her father.

"Oh?" Annabel had caught the nuance of the unspoken remark. "Who do you favor as victim, then?"

Leonora winced. That had been a most unfortunate word for Annabel to choose.

Annabel didn't miss the wince, either. Leonora was beginning to understand why the others thought Annabel was a dangerous person to have around in a crisis.

"See here—" A crafty glint had appeared in Annabel's narrowed eyes. "I came over to get you and bring you back for drinks. So come along now. Got a nice pitcher of fresh martinis chilling in the fridge."

"Oh, I can't!" Leonora knew that she was in far too weakened a condition to face drinks with Annabel in an inquisitive mood. Annabel's martinis were strong enough to make a stone statue confess to carrying on with the pigeons.

"Why not?" Now Annabel was more suspicious than ever. "Packed it in for the day, haven't you?"

"Painting, yes." Leonora discovered that she had. "But I have the housework to catch up with—"

"Leave it for the cleaning woman. They *have* lined up Ruby for you, haven't they?"

"I don't know. Bunty mentioned it when I first arrived, but I haven't heard any more about it—"

"Bunty is a busy gel," Annabel said drily. "So much to think about that it takes her a while to get round to things."

"And, of course, I haven't been here all that long yet . . ." It was beginning to seem like a lifetime. Leonora yawned suddenly.

"You see? You're exhausted. Mustn't flog yourself any more today. Tell you what, I'll get the pitcher of martinis and bring it over here."

"Oh, I'm sorry—" Leonora thought fast. "Ordinarily, that would be fine, but . . . I'm expecting an overseas call. Rather a private one—it's going to be long and complicated . . ."

"Oh . . ." Even Annabel couldn't linger after that. "Next time, then." She moved towards the door, tacitly admitting defeat—or, at least, a tactical setback.

"I'll see you at the luncheon tomorrow," Leonora said.

The pre-luncheon drinking must have started a considerable time before Leonora's arrival. She found herself immediately backed into a corner by one of the young male houseguests, who proceeded to lecture at length on a subject undoubtedly near to his heart. Unfortunately, she only managed to understand about one word in ten; the other nine were just a sort of gurgle at the back of his throat. After the first few moments of panic, she realized that it didn't matter whether she understood him or not. He was not going to ask her any questions; he was totally uninterested in her opinions, he was merely giving her the benefit of his.

Relaxing, Leonora looked around the drawing-room, remembering to nod occasionally. There were quite a few faces she didn't know and several familiar ones. Some people sent her sympathetic smiles as they recognized her plight, but no one moved to her rescue. They were obviously relieved that she was diverting her unwelcome partner's attention from themselves.

But not for long, Leonora promised herself, nodding once again. Bunty was in a far corner of the room, earnestly discussing something with Phil Mottram and two people Leonora had not yet met. If Bunty's attitude was anything to go by, she was not likely to meet them. Bunty was carefully not looking in her direction and, when she obviously felt that she was being watched, she shifted her position slightly so that her back was to the room.

Leonora was beginning to feel that her own back was to the wall. Eddie was standing by the drinks table with Tessa Andrews and another woman, obviously willing to play the genial host to everyone but Leonora.

There was nothing like discovering a dead body to make you extremely unpopular.

Molly emerged from the back of the house carrying a tray of cocktail sausages and vol-au-vents. She faltered in mid-stride at seeing Leonora. Leonora smiled brightly at her.

Molly returned a sickly smile, then noticed James Abercorn standing nearby brooding into his drink. She caught him by the shoulder, spoke urgently for a moment, thrust the tray into his hands and gave him a push in Leonora's direction. He ambled over reluctantly. Molly disappeared into the back of the house.

"Umm . . . the sausages are rather good." James thrust the tray at her and looked hopeful, perhaps hoping she would take the tray from him.

"Ah, thanks very much." Her partner became momentarily comprehensible at the sight of food. "Awff'ly decent of you, old boy." He took two sausages, three vol-au-vents and settled down to clearing the tray.

James stood there, clutching the tray with both hands and looking helpless. He had not quite the nerve to walk away with it.

"See here, old boy—" Mouth full, which didn't improve his diction, the man transferred his attention from the depleted tray to James. "Where's your drink?"

"Oh, er . . . over there." James indicated the general direction with a twitch of his head. He had set down his drink on the corner of a table when Molly had pushed the tray at him.

"Can't have that. Stay here—get you a fresh one." Impelled to generosity by the fact that his own glass was empty, the man patted James on the shoulder and went towards the drinks table.

"No, really—I've had enough," James called after him.

"No such thing's enough. Specially when old Eddie's paying." He was shouldering his way to the drinks.

"But I don't want—" James broke off, realizing it was no use. "Here—" he turned back to Leonora with the tray— "take something before that Oink hogs it all."

"Oink?" She hadn't expected James to be so graphic. Surprised, Leonora took a vol-au-vent absently.

"That's what they call themselves," James said savagely. "Stands for One Income, No Kids. OINK, you see? Very fitting, too, I might add."

"Perhaps we can slip away before he gets back," Leonora suggested.

James brightened and turned to lead the way, then turned back, dejected. "Too late."

"Here we are—three of the best." The Oink had returned, clutching three over-full glasses with liquid slopping down their sides. He distributed them like largesse.

With a sinking heart, Leonora recognized the clear fluid of Annabel's lethal martinis.

Having done what he considered his duty by Leonora, the Oink concentrated on James. For once, Leonora blessed the male chauvinism that meant an audience of their own sex was preferred and began to edge away.

James watched her go with a wistful gaze. His eyes were already glazing with boredom and perhaps the effects of Annabel's martini, which he had begun sipping mechanically.

Leonora headed for the doorway through which she had seen Molly disappear. As she reached it, she nearly collided with Clio, who was coming through with a platter of canapés.

"Don't tell me they've pressed you into service already," Clio greeted her. "I thought you were still in the honeymoon stage." She glanced meaningly towards Bunty and Eddie.

"The honeymoon is over." Leonora was thinking of yesterday, but Clio couldn't know that. She put her own interpretation on the remark.

"You'd better report to the kitchen, then. They're setting up the buffet in the dining-room—and it's all hands to the pump. The County Set will be arriving any minute."

The doorbell rang and Leonora glanced over her shoulder to see Bunty and Eddie move forward in unison. A shrill babble of greetings rang in her ears as she continued in what she hoped was the direction of the kitchen. Clio swerved around her and headed for the thick of the party bearing the platter before her.

The kitchen wasn't where she had thought it would be. The corridor ended in a large pleasant sitting-room with French windows which opened on to a grey-flagstoned terrace where several strangers laughed and held out their glasses as Annabel dispensed martinis from an ornate jug. Leonora retreated and tried again.

This time she took a different turning along the corridor and tried another door. She found herself in a small cloakroom and took advantage of it by pouring her over-strong drink down the drain and replacing it with clear water. It looked exactly the same and some judicious sipping should enable her to eke out the counterfeit until it was time to graduate to the buffet.

She never did discover what the next door led into. The crescendo of giggles and squeals sent her into rapid retreat, closing the door behind her as quietly as she could.

She found herself back in the drawing-room just in time to see the Oink pressing yet another martini upon poor James, who was shaking his head in demur even as his hand closed around the brimming glass. The party was in full swing.

People she had never seen before—and some she hoped never to see again—were milling about, shrieking at each other. No one seemed to be listening.

"There you are!" Before she could back away, a hand closed on her arm and she was drawn into a corner. "I've been looking for you. I thought you'd be here today."

"Oh." About to pull away, Leonora recognized her captor. "It's Mr. Mottram, isn't it?"

"Phil, please." He looked at her earnestly. "And you're Leonora, I hear. A damned good sport."

"Aren't you going to introduce me to your friend, Phil?" Tessa Andrews materialized at his elbow, frowning.

"You've already met," Phil said. "Although I'm not sure you were in any shape to remember it."

"Oh yes—" Tessa's face cleared. "You were one of the people who came to help when I had my little argument with the gatepost. You're the new tenant in the gardener's cottage."

"That's right." Leonora looked at her curiously; she had said "gardener" without an apparent qualm. Perhaps Tessa really was innocent of his death. Or, if she had been responsible, she had not noticed it.

"Hello, Leonora." Suddenly Bunty had joined the group, acknowledging Leonora's presence for the first time. "So glad you could come. Where's Mummy?"

"I haven't seen her—" Leonora began, but the question had not been addressed to her. Already, Bunty was looking past her for an answer.

"Don't know," Phil said. "I thought she was doing something about the buffet. Ordering the servants around, maybe."

"I hope not," Bunty said. "I wouldn't like them to give notice."

"I thought I saw her going downstairs earlier," Tessa said.

"Oh, *not* the kitchen!" Bunty sighed in exasperation. "Giles is overseeing things down there. He's the only one who doesn't upset Cook."

"Someone's in the kitchen with Dinah—" a wag behind them chanted, and guffawed loudly.

In the distance, James accepted another drink. He had given up protesting; his movements were as stiff and mechanical as those of a robot.

Leonora jumped as a gong crashed somewhere behind her.

"Luncheon is served," Bunty called out loudly. "In the dining-room." She led the way down the hall and into a long room where a table nearly as long as the room was laden with an impressive array of salads and cold meats. At each end of the table, chafing dishes bubbled with chicken à la king and bœuf Stroganoff.

With shrieks of delight, the guests swarmed over the food like famished locusts.

"I still don't see Mummy," Bunty complained.

Molly and Giles were also among the missing, Leonora noted; but just then Phil passed her a heaped plate and she found herself part of his group being shepherded down to the far end of the room. The dining-room led into the sitting-room she had discovered earlier and some people were carrying their plates through to the terrace beyond.

The noise level fell as the guests attacked their food, then rose again in the interval before returning to the table for refills or the sweet course.

Idly, Leonora noticed that the Oink had remained down by the door. She was watching him as he lifted his head from the trough and wrinkled his nose.

"I say," he called out. "Does anyone smell smoke?"

CHAPTER 10

Eddie was nearest the door. He gave a grimace obviously intended to be a reassuring smile, turned on his heel and dashed for the drawing-room.

"Someone's left a cigarette smoldering." Bunty gave her assessment of the situation without moving, but her gaze raked the room, searching for someone who was not to be found. "Has anyone seen Mummy?"

"Giles!" Out in the entrance hall, Eddie was calling for reinforcements.

"Is it serious? Can we help?" A couple of the guests caught up seltzer bottles and headed for the excitement.

"Call the Fire Brigade," someone else suggested.

"It's nothing serious," Bunty insisted. "Eddie can take care of it."

No one asked her how she could know since she had not stirred from her chair since the Oink sounded the alarm, but several sceptical glances were aimed in her direction and some of the more nervous guests drifted towards the sitting-room and the terrace, ready to get well clear of the house if an emergency developed.

"Perhaps I ought to go and see if I can do anything." Phil

stood up, but Tessa grabbed his arm, pulling him back.

"Eddie will tell us soon enough if he needs help," she said. "Sit down before you start a panic."

The smell of smoke was becoming more noticeable and the exodus towards the terrace was gaining momentum. It would not be many moments before they were the only ones left in the dining-room. Leonora felt that she would be far happier on the terrace herself, but could not make the first move while Tessa and Phil and Bunty were being so stiff-upper-lippish about the situation.

"Such a flap!" Bunty glanced dismissively at those edging towards the terrace. "People get so nervous over every little thing these days."

Leonora wondered just what it would take to make Bunty nervous. A corpse in the grounds hadn't done it, now she was rising above a fire in the building. Nerves of steel—or an inadequate assessment of life's problems?

"Don't you think it might be a good idea to call the Fire Department?" Leonora suggested.

"Whatever for?" Bunty gave her a look of open dislike. She was being a troublemaker again. "Eddie and Giles will have everything under control by now."

"You make this sound like a regular occurrence." Tessa was amused. If she didn't watch her step, she was going to be marked down as a troublemaker, too. If she hadn't been already. Someone who had nearly written off the gatepost, if not the ex-gardener, could not be completely in her hostess's good books.

"These things happen," Bunty said vaguely. "There's always someone in every group who's careless with a cigarette."

"What extraordinary groups you must entertain," Tessa said. "Quite a few of my friends smoke, but no one has ever started a fire yet."

"Let's hope that 'yet' isn't the operative word." Phil glanced uneasily at Leonora, aware that his excuse for invading her cottage the other day was being shown up as a lie.

"Can I get you some coffee, everyone?" He changed the subject determinedly, something not easy to do with wisps of smoke curling through the atmosphere.

"I'll have mine on the terrace," Leonora said firmly, giving up the struggle to be diplomatic. If Bunty wanted to commit social suttee, that was her business—she was the hostess, after all. The guests had no need to follow her example.

"What a good idea." Tessa was right behind her. "I could do with a breath of fresh air."

Their exit was the signal for the remaining stragglers, some of whom were coughing slightly, to evacuate the dining-room. Even Bunty, after a forbidding frown, surrendered and regrouped with her guests on the terrace under the guise of giving Phil a helping hand with the coffee.

Some of the guests had already found the way down to the lawn below the terrace and were strolling towards the front of the house to see what was happening. Leonora wished that she could join them, but Bunty's presence prevented that.

"Why don't we shut the door?" Phil looked around restively. "The draught could be dangerous. You don't want the whole house going up."

"Don't be silly," Bunty said. "Everything must be all right by now." She frowned with sudden uneasiness. "Otherwise, Eddie would have called for help."

"Maybe he's too busy fighting the fire." Phil leaned over, stretched out a hand and swung the French windows shut. "You've got a nice house here, you wouldn't like to see it go up in flames, would you?"

"No—" Bunty glanced at him oddly. "No, I wouldn't." She started towards the French window. "Perhaps I ought to go and find out what's happening."

"Not that way!" Phil stopped her. "If the fire's spreading, you could get caught in it."

"Perhaps you're right." Bunty changed course, heading for the steps at the end of the terrace.

"Damn right I'm right," Phil growled. "And I'll come with you, too, before you try to do anything else stupid."

Bunty gave him another odd look, but neither rebuked nor rebuffed him. They moved away, not quite in step.

"Wait a minute," Tessa said. "I'm coming, too. There might be something I can do."

Leonora trailed after them. They had not been the only ones with that idea. The terrace was nearly deserted, the guests having left to circle the house in search of excitement. From some of the laughing phrases that drifted back to her, she got the impression that a few ungrateful guests would find it quite amusing to be witnesses to a conflagration. She noticed that Bunty's strides had lengthened irritably and she wondered if Bunty could identify the voices; they might find themselves struck off future guest lists.

The front of the house looked as gracious and peaceful as ever. It was only when one drew closer that something appeared subtly wrong about the vaulted windows of the drawing-room. They were marked by streaks of soot and several of the mullioned panes were cracked.

"It's all right," Eddie was assuring the first arrivals. "No problem. The drapes caught fire, that's all. It's out now. There was never any danger." Over their heads, his eyes sought Bunty's, a slightly different message in them for her.

Behind him, someone began swinging open the windows and wisps of dark smoke drifted out into the air to disperse. As the final frame swung open, there was a brilliant flash and Leonora tensed, thinking the fire had broken out afresh. Then she was aware that it was just Annabel's diamonds as the sunlight struck sparks from them. Trust Annabel to be in the thick of the action.

On the lawn at the far side of the house, Clio, Molly and Giles were clustered around James, who was nearly as soot-streaked as Eddie and looked shaken but still glassy-eyed.

"There!" Lady Cosgreave appeared in the doorway. "The place is airing out nicely. We'll give it about another half-hour before we go back in, I think."

"Actually—" one of the "County Set" said briskly—"it's time for me to be getting along anyway."

There was a general murmur of agreement from the guests who were not members of the houseparty. They began to disperse as quickly as the smoke, their departure marked by the slamming of car doors and shouts of farewell.

"I'm glad it's no worse than it is." Phil surveyed the front of the manor house assessingly. "No real damage done, is there?"

"Nothing to speak of," Eddie said grimly. "We were thinking about getting new drapes anyhow."

"Oh, well—" Tessa gave a little giggle. "Bang goes another no-claims bonus!"

"Oh, it won't come to that." Eddie frowned at her. "I don't think we'll bother about a little thing like this. Bunty's been looking for an excuse to redecorate. Now she's got it."

The words were light, but his eyes were shadowed. For a wild instant Leonora wondered whether Bunty might have started the fire deliberately so that they would have to redecorate. Then she remembered that Bunty had been at the buffet in the dining-room when the fire started.

Or rather, when everyone had first become aware of it. That smoldering cigarette Bunty had been so insistent about could have been left too close to the drapes quite a long time before that. And Bunty *was* a smoker.

"Still, it's tough luck," Phil said. Another smoker. Where had he left his last cigarette? Had he stubbed it out thoroughly? From the expression on his face, he might be wondering that himself. He was already on the defensive about smoking in front of Eddie—had there, perhaps, been an earlier incident?

"No use worrying about it." Eddie shrugged. "Not much harm done. Nothing we can't handle."

"Eddie—" Annabel came up to them, rubbing her red-rimmed eyes and blinking. "I'm afraid the rug is scorched where a bit of the drape fell on it. I've moved the end table to cover it."

"There!" Tessa said. "Now you'll *have* to report it to the insurance company. It will cost a bomb to repair that rug."

"Maybe we'll just get a new rug instead." Eddie gave her a look of cold dislike. "We'd have to, anyway, if Bunty changes the color scheme."

"It's not that serious." Tessa did not seem to be popular with Annabel, either. "Once the place is cleared out—" Leonora had the impression that Annabel was referring to the guests and not to the smoke—"Eddie can take a good look at it and they'll probably be able to do something about it. Just a good brushing would help. Meanwhile, I've got the table over it so that the soot won't get trodden in."

"Sure," Eddie said. "No need to fuss. It takes a few burns and scratches to give a home that lived-in look." He turned and looked at the house with more affection than he had bestowed on any of them. "This old house has seen worse than this throughout the centuries."

Annabel coughed abruptly and turned away. Leonora remembered her statement that the house was a Victorian fake. It sounded as though Eddie did not know that. The place had not been standing through so many centuries as he fondly supposed. Just over one, in fact.

"Have a glass of milk," Eddie told Annabel. "That's good for smoke inhalation. It will soothe that cough."

"Thank you." Annabel dabbed at her eyes again. "I'll do that . . . in a minute or two." She looked at the group at the far side of the lawn. "First, I want to make sure James is all right."

Leonora slipped away from her companions and followed after Annabel. They did not appear to notice that she had left them, nor Annabel that she had joined her. Nevertheless, she trotted in Annabel's wake, opting for the devils she knew . . .

What an unsettling thought! Where had that come from? There was nothing particularly devilish about Clio, Molly, Giles and James. If anything, they were . . . what? Not angels, certainly. Victims? No . . . but . . . She slowed her steps, trying to identify value judgments she had not been aware of forming.

Annabel had already reached her friends. Uneasily, Leonora quickened her steps, feeling that she had crossed some invisible Rubicon. She had thrown in her lot with these strangers, rather than with Bunty, Eddie and their crowd. Even when she paused to think about it, she did not regret the fact, but she still found it unsettling. Why should she be forced to choose at all?

"How is James?" Annabel was asking quietly as she came up to the little group.

"Still quite shaken," Molly replied. "I don't think he's taken it in yet."

"It was quite a shock for him, poor fellow," Giles said. "He couldn't have realized—" He glanced at Leonora and broke off.

"Did James discover the fire?" she asked.

"He tried to put it out all by himself," Molly said. "Look at his hands. If he'll just come back with me, I'll bandage them and give him something for shock."

"Shouldn't we call a doctor?" Leonora already suspected what the answer to that was going to be. She had never seen such a self-sufficient community.

"We don't need one," Giles said quickly. "Molly can do everything necessary. She's trained for it and our medicine cabinet is better equipped than some pharmacies."

"But we ought to get him moving," Molly said. "Giles, see what you can do—he's rooted to the spot."

"Right. Come on, James—" Giles put an arm around James, trying to urge him forward. "Let's go and get you seen to."

"I'm all right, I'm all right." Shoulders hunched, James stood immovable. His head rolled to one side, his eyes seemed to be trying to focus on something in the distance. "Is the fire out? Are Bunty and Eddie furious?"

"All's well, don't worry about it." Giles tried again to move him, but James continued to balk. "Come along . . ."

"Oh, poor James!" Clio quivered with distress. "*Look* at his hands. Help him, for heaven's sake, help him."

"Damn it, woman, we're trying to!" Giles snapped. "Why don't you go and boil a kettle—or something."

"There's no need to be rude." Clio was injured.

"And no need for you to get so upset," Annabel said brusquely. "He's not the first person around here to get his fingers burned."

"You *would* say that!" Clio turned on her heel and stalked away.

"James—" Giles shook him lightly. "Come along, James. Excitement over. Time to treat the wounded. Come along."

James remained rigid. He appeared to see and hear nothing.

"James, you're being extremely tiresome!" Annabel spoke in a no-nonsense voice. She tapped him sharply on the wrist— a tap that was just short of being a slap. "Go with Molly and get those hands seen to."

"Oh . . . um . . . ah . . ." James creaked slowly back to life. "What . . . ?" He blinked, yawned, stretched—and was suddenly racked with pain from his incautiously exercised hands. "Ow!"

"Come along—" Giles swung him about, heading him towards the East Wing. "We'll see you right." They moved off together.

"Good girl, Annabel!" Molly said before hurrying after them. "You sounded just like a school matron."

"I intended to," Annabel said. "I thought that would get through to James."

"It certainly did," Leonora said, watching Molly and Giles steer James towards their wing.

"Matron's word is law," Annabel said, "even to the schoolmasters. It's part of the mystique of the Old School Tie—comes in jolly useful sometimes. They'd have been all night trying to shift James, otherwise."

"I still think he should see a doctor," Leonora said. "What if those hands turn septic?"

"Then we'll get him to a doctor. Not before. Don't worry. Molly's very good at this sort of thing. He'll be all right."

"Yes, I know. She said she used to be a nurse before she married Giles."

"Did she?" Annabel raised a disbelieving eyebrow. "I doubt that."

"You mean she wasn't a nurse? But why should she lie about it? And Giles says they have a professional medicine cabinet. Anyway, I don't—" Leonora broke off, trying to think of a tactful way to say that it didn't bother her if Molly wished to upgrade her professional qualifications.

"Never mind." Annabel looked across at the others and smiled oddly. "Why don't we say goodbye to our host and hostess? I think the party's over. At least, for us."

The remaining members of the houseparty looked as though they wished it were over for them, too. Still clutching half-drained cups of coffee or empty plates, they milled about on the lawn, looking wistful as yet another car escaped down the driveway.

"Oh yes, goodbye." Bunty accepted their thanks and fare-wells absently. "Sorry about all the flap." She grimaced at them and drifted off to talk to some of her remaining guests before Leonora could add anything more.

"Is James okay?" Only Eddie appeared to be concerned about the man who had tried to extinguish the fire.

"Molly's taking care of him," Annabel said. "He'll be well enough by morning. Except for his hands—and his hang-over."

"Yeah, well—" Eddie was on the defensive, seeming to find criticism in the innocent words. "I couldn't keep an eye on him every minute. How was I to know he was knocking back so much? He's usually awfully good about it."

"I'm afraid he fell in with uncongenial company," Annabel said. "Boredom will do it every time. And perhaps," she added ruefully, "I made the martinis too strong. Perhaps I ought to put ice in them."

"Never!" Eddie laughed out loud and patted her shoulder. "You just keep on doing things the way you always do. You're just great, Annabel—don't ever change."

"I don't plan to," Annabel said tartly. "But you'd better watch your guests more closely in future."

"Okay, it's a deal." Eddie was still grinning. Until he glanced over their shoulders and his expression changed.

Leonora looked around in time to see Bunty link arms with Phil Mottram and disappear around the side of the house. Tessa, left behind, glared after them.

"Excuse me," Eddie said. "I ought to—" He began to move away.

"I'll see you in the morning," Leonora reminded him. "First thing."

"Huh?" He stopped and stared at her in bewilderment.

She stared back, trying to put as much meaning as possible into her stare.

"Oh," he said. "Oh, yeah. Well, maybe not *first* thing. Tell you what, why don't you come up for lunch and we'll talk things over."

"But—"

"Gotta go. Sorry." Eddie turned and dashed away, leaving Leonora with Annabel staring at her quizzically.

"You're *not* getting mixed up in one of his 'financial arrangements'?" It was as much an accusation as a question. "Not after I warned you—"

"No, no," Leonora said. "Nothing like that." And realized, too late, that she had been trapped into having to provide some sort of explanation of what it *was* like.

Annabel waited patiently.

"I'll tell you later," Leonora said firmly, promising herself that "later" wasn't going to come. She began to walk back towards her cottage, which was also unsatisfactory, as Annabel fell into step beside her.

"All right," Annabel agreed unconvincingly. They walked in silence for a moment, then she said, "Come in and have a cup of coffee . . . and perhaps a liqueur. Our luncheon was rather disrupted. Did you get to the sweet stage? I may have something in the fridge."

"Oh dear, I'd love to," Leonora said, equally unconvincingly, "but I'm afraid I'm expecting an overseas call—another one." She had used the excuse before, but there was nothing to say that she did not receive a constant stream of overseas calls. After all, as a supposed widow, it could be presumed that there was an estate to be settled.

"Of course." Annabel surrendered with good grace. "Another time, perhaps?"

"Definitely." Leonora smiled as Annabel took the turning to her own cottage. She watched, slowing her steps until she was almost motionless, until Annabel disappeared into the cottage with a final backward wave.

Bending as though to clear a bit of weed from the edge of the driveway, Leonora counted to twenty slowly, then continued on her way. Then, with frequent surreptitious glances over her shoulder to make sure that she was unobserved, she detoured around by the bushes near the gatepost.

It took another few minutes of simulated weed-clearing until she had gathered her courage enough to creep underneath the branches. Still another until she could open her eyes and stare about her.

She needn't have worried. The body was gone.

CHAPTER 11

The body was not only not there but, in the dim light filtering through the branches, it looked as though a body never had been there.

Even more unsettling, it *did* look as though a gardener had been there. A live gardener. The earth beneath the bush had been cleared of all dead leaves and branches and the marks of a rake were clearly to be discerned.

Had Horton merely been unconscious and, embarrassed and wishing to eradicate any traces of his weakness, tidied away all evidence that he had lain beneath the bush?

Leonora crouched beneath the fanned-out branches, irresolute. She had not had the courage to creep under the branches and see for herself. One look at that protruding foot had been enough for her. She regretted her cowardice now; now that it was too late.

But Bunty and Eddie had also viewed the body and had had no doubt that there was one. A dead one. They had bent all their efforts to keep her from calling the police. They would not have done that if there had been nothing for the police to find but a man sleeping off the effects of too much drink.

She became aware of a cramp in her leg and began to edge back towards the driveway beyond the overhanging branches. As she did so, a car raced past with a bad-tempered roar, so close that it seemed a miracle that it had not hit her. She jumped, startled, and her hair caught and tangled in the dead twigs above her.

Trapped, she crouched again, fighting down panic and trying not to think of things like skeletal hands reaching out to clutch her. She took a deep breath and reached up to work her hair free.

It was well and truly snarled into the twigs. She tugged sharply, then stopped, appalled at the thought of what she might bring down upon her head.

But that was ridiculous. She forced herself to look up into the tangle of branches, twigs and leaves; they were not strong enough to support the weight of a body. Nor could a body be hidden up there, the foliage was not thick enough. It was only here in the clearing around the bole where the children had fashioned themselves a leafy cave that there was room enough to store and conceal a body.

Another car screamed past the gatepost, expensive engine snarling as it dashed to freedom like a wild animal loosed from a cage. From up at the Hall she could hear a fresh shriek of farewells and the mocking salute of a horn as someone else prepared to make his getaway.

That settled it. This was not the sort of hiding-place someone would creep into to sleep off his liquor. Especially not if there was any danger of awakening with a hangover. He might as well settle himself down at a crossroads in rush hour. He would not have chosen this spot voluntarily.

Someone else had placed him here. Or else he had been hurled here by the collision with Tessa's car just as she struck the gatepost. In the resultant turmoil, no one had noticed or suspected that another human being could have been involved in the accident. All the interest, all the sympathy, had centered on Tessa and her damaged vehicle.

But he hadn't got up and walked away by himself. The man was dead. Molly had said so and Molly had no reason to lie.

The expressions on the faces of Bunty and Eddie were further proof that what they had seen beneath the bush had not just been a figment of Molly's imagination. Nor her own.

Nor were the efforts they had made to discourage her from reporting the body to the police. She had thought they were delaying action until the party ended; now she knew the real reason for the delay. They had removed the body and there were no prizes for guessing that they would deny that there had ever been one.

She jerked angrily at her hair and it came free. Her scalp stung and throbbed. Ignoring the pain, she parted the branches and emerged on to the tiny strip of lawn separating the bush from the driveway.

What had they done with the body? Bunty had recommended taking him back to the pub and leaving him there. Had they done it? Or were they waiting until the houseparty ended and all the guests had escaped back to their own safe protected lives?

But Bunty and Eddie were even more concerned to save and protect their own skins. Having covered up the death and removed the body to some neutral ground, were they now about to call the police, as they had promised her, first thing in the morning and attempt to sort out the problem? There were no prizes for guessing the answer to that one, either.

The police in America would look most unfavorably on people who readjusted the scene of an accident to their own advantage. There was no reason to suppose that the English police would view the matter any differently. Especially when the victim had been carried away and—

And what? What had they done with the body?

Thrown it in the river? Hidden it in a real cave? Buried it? To what lengths would Eddie go to protect his precious Tessa?

It was surprising that Giles had allowed himself to be involved in such a thing. Involved? He must have been an

active participant. Eddie would have needed help to dispose of
the body and she could not see Bunty taking the head or heels
of the corpse and helping to carry it to its new resting-place.
No, Giles was in it up to his neck.

Molly, too, could not be unaware of what had been done. No
wonder she had avoided Leonora at the luncheon party. It was
Molly, in fact, who had prevented her from notifying the
police in the first place and insisted that Eddie had to be told
about it before anyone else. Molly must have had a good idea
of what Eddie's reaction would be.

Leonora marched across the driveway and up to the door of
her cottage—the ex-gardener's ex-tied cottage—the ramrod
stiffness of her back and the tightness of her lips boding ill for
those who had deceived her. She would telephone the Hall and
demand explanations—and action.

They sent Lady Cosgreave down to deal with her.

Dinah, Lady Cosgreave, entered, smiling falsely. The smile
quickly grew thin and faded, to be replaced by an icy frown.

"I really can't see what you expect us to do about it," Lady
Cosgreave said coldly.

"Do about it?" The effrontery of it took Leonora's breath
away. "You—*they*—have done too much already. They've got
to return the body, report it to the police—"

"What body?" Lady Cosgreave asked.

"Horton's—Molly said it was Horton. Your ex-gardener."

"Indeed?" Lady Cosgreave arched a disbelieving eyebrow.
"And when did Molly say this?"

"When we found the body. She crawled under the bush and
inspected it. Head wounds, she said. It could have happened
when Tessa's car ran into the gatepost. A glancing blow—"

"I think you'll find," Lady Cosgreave said, "that Molly
and Giles share a rather primitive sense of humor. I'm afraid
you've been the victim of an elaborate practical joke."

"No," Leonora said. "I don't believe that."

"I am not accustomed to being called a liar!"

"I am not accustomed to being treated like a child!"

They faced each other in open hostility. Lady Cosgreave was the first to gather the shreds of her social manner around herself again. She bestowed a forgiving smile on Leonora.

"I understand that you did not actually see this alleged body yourself."

"I saw the foot," Leonora said reluctantly. "The dead foot. Sticking out from under the bush."

"Quite so. You saw a foot. But you did not investigate further . . . not personally?"

"Not then . . ." Leonora was on the defensive and resented it. "Molly was with me and she moved so fast. She was under the bush before I could move. And there wasn't room for two under there. I mean . . . for three." The memory of that cramped clearing shrouded by overhanging branches returned to her and she shuddered.

"Ah yes," Lady Cosgreave said. "You've viewed the . . . scene, this afternoon, haven't you?"

"I wanted to see for myself . . ." Why had it taken her so long to get up enough courage to investigate? That was the weakest part of her case.

"But there was nothing to see." Lady Cosgreave finished for her, with elaborate patience.

"There *had* been. Molly will tell them—"

"I think not."

They stared at each other: stalemate.

"It should be reported," Leonora said stubbornly.

"There is nothing to report." Lady Cosgreave was equally stubborn.

"But—"

"You have no *corpus delicti* to produce. If you tell such a story—and offer no proof at all—" Lady Cosgreave shrugged dismissively. "I'm afraid the police would not be very happy about it. They don't like people who waste their time. And, if they chose to, they could make life rather difficult for you, I'm afraid."

"Difficult . . ." Leonora echoed faintly, already suspecting what was coming.

"They might just wonder," Lady Cosgreave hinted delicately, "whether you were . . . entirely reliable. I mean, you *are* an artist . . . a foreigner . . . a female . . . and you've claimed to be a widow. If they investigate at all, the first thing they'll discover is that you weren't . . . entirely truthful about that."

"But you told me to say I was a widow!" Leonora gasped.

"Did I? I really can't remember. In any case, it's not important. They will discover that, for whatever reasons of your own, you told everyone that you were widowed when you were actually divorced—and that will cast doubt on everything else you claim."

"I see." They would find out more than that. They would find out that she had never been married, and so could never have been divorced, either. Any probing into her past and they would decide that she was a fantasist at best—a pathological liar at worst. She was in a no-win situation. Lady Cosgreave didn't know the half of it.

"I was sure you'd understand the position once it was made clear to you," Lady Cosgreave said smoothly.

"It's getting clearer by the minute," Leonora said.

"Of course, we understand that you've been going through a very difficult time." Lady Cosgreave was prepared to be magnanimous. "It isn't surprising that you're overwrought. Many people would have had a nervous breakdown long before this."

So now she was mentally unstable!

"And, my dear, you must never forget that you're a foreigner. A stranger in this country, with no one to look after you in case of illness—" Lady Cosgreave had failed to notice that she had rounded a dangerous corner and reached the point where her massed arguments were becoming counter-productive.

"I'm not likely to forget that." The flash in Leonora's eyes might have unsettled Lady Cosgreave, had she been watching. "I've just had a crash course in remembering."

"Only in your own best interests, my dear. We wouldn't want you to find yourself in . . . unpleasant circumstances."

"And I suppose your friend, the Chief Constable, would also share your views."

"Hereward?" Lady Cosgreave looked startled at the sudden intrusion of another aspect of the situation. "Hereward is the dearest, sweetest gentleman in the world. Naturally, he would not wish to upset someone who was already . . . rather disturbed."

"Perhaps you'd like me to leave," Leonora said bluntly. "Tear up the tenancy agreement and clear out."

"Oh no, no! I never thought of such a thing!" Lady Cosgreave, perhaps foreseeing a request for a refund of the unexpired rent, now gave every indication of being most disturbed herself. "No one was thinking of such a thing for one moment. All we want is for you to be reasonable."

Leonora stood silent for a moment. The silence seemed to further unnerve Lady Cosgreave.

"You're happy here, aren't you?" she asked. "You've been working well? You get along with everyone? They like you, you know. It would be pity to throw it all away just because . . ."

Leonora waited. *Because you believe in justice? Because you found a dead body and believe the police should know about it? Because you resent being bullied and threatened, however subtly?*

" . . . because of a silly misunderstanding," Lady Cosgreave finished, looking off into the distance. It had been some time since she had looked Leonora in the eye.

"I would," Leonora agreed slowly, "hate to disrupt my

work at this point." Moreover, she couldn't afford to. Her deadline was looming ahead; if she hadn't completed enough canvases for an exhibition, the opportunity might be given to someone else. Or she might have to share the exhibition with another artist, which would be unsatisfactory for both of them.

"Then you must stay and get on with your work." Lady Cosgreave's smile flared like a signal beacon. "A very wise decision, my dear, and one I'm sure you'll never regret."

Leonora was regretting it already, but could see no alternative. They held all the cards—including the body. She would only make a fool of herself if she pursued the problem. They were all obviously prepared to lie themselves blue in the face—and blacken her own reputation at the same time. Although art dealers paid homage to Van Gogh, they were not too keen on the idea of having a deranged living artist in a position to haunt their galleries. A little light eccentricity was as much as they were willing to bargain for. Someone who hallucinated dead bodies would not find a ready welcome.

"You spoke of Hereward—you must meet him." In triumph, Lady Cosgreave was prepared to be even more magnanimous. "Come to dinner—"

"Not tonight," Leonora said hastily. She needed more time to think over the situation.

"Of course, not tonight," Lady Cosgreave agreed. "You're so overtired. You need to rest. Tuesday—he's coming to dinner on Tuesday. You must join us."

"I . . ." Leonora hesitated, unable to produce a sufficiently convincing excuse on the spur of the moment.

"You've already met his daughter, I believe," Lady Cosgreave said. "She was here this weekend. Dear Tessa."

CHAPTER 12

"Uncle Herry, darling!" Bunty squealed with girlish (perhaps too girlish?) delight and hurled herself into the arms of the tall, heavy-set and quite distinguished-looking man who had just entered the sitting-room.

"Little Bunty!" His arms circled her waist and he gave her several pats (perhaps too far down?) on the back.

With jaundiced eyes, Leonora watched the touching scene.

"Hereward—my dear!" Lady Cosgreave swept forward to be kissed on both cheeks.

"Hereward—good to see you!" Annabel, too, was greeted with some warmth. Just one big happy circle of friends.

The tribal intimacies having been established, Bunty performed the introductions to the rest of the group. It was a small dinner-party; only Leonora and Phil Mottram were strangers. James seemed to have a nodding acquaintance with the guest of honor, established at some earlier meeting. Leonora suspected that James was often pressed into service as an extra man at Bunty's dinner-parties to balance her table.

James stood beside Leonora, nursing a glass of Perrier water, with the brooding expression that seemed to be habitual. Probably he would much rather be at home by his own fireside, reading a history book or plotting out the next chess move in one of those long-distance games conducted by post.

For that matter, she would prefer to be at home herself, even washing paint brushes or sizing canvases. But Dinah had telephoned that morning to remind her of the dinner and Annabel had called round to collect her and walk up the drive with her. It had been neatly arranged so that she had had no chance to change her mind.

"So nice to see you, my dear." Lady Cosgreave had deigned to notice her presence. "Are you feeling better?"

"I feel fine," Leonora said. "I've been working." She had stayed inside the cottage since Sunday evening, repulsing all efforts to draw her out. She wasn't sure whether Annabel had quite forgiven her for refusing an invitation to drinks; she knew that Clio had been upset and disappointed when she rejected another kind offer of a drive in a different direction and a shopping tour of towns on the other side of the river. Not surprisingly, Molly and Giles had not contacted her at all.

"Eddie hasn't been feeling too well the past couple of days," Bunty said. She gave a sudden bray of laughter. "I hope it was nothing I served at the luncheon."

"I wasn't ill," Leonora said. "I've been working." But no one was paying any attention.

"Couldn't be that." Phil rushed in to reassure Bunty. "I'm all right, you and Dinah are all right. How about you, James, you been feeling okay?"

"Oh, er—" James looked hideously embarrassed. The others waited for his reply; they seemed to have forgotten that he never actually got to the buffet that afternoon. "Er, yes, except for my hands—and I had a frightful hangover next day."

"That was Annabel's martinis," Bunty hooted.

"Yes, well . . ." James looked into his glass of Perrier water. "I'm planning to be more abstemious from now on."

"You don't have to worry tonight," Eddie said. "There are no martinis on offer. Not that we don't think they're great, Annabel," he added hastily. "But tonight we're sticking with wine. Wait until you see what I've found." He turned to Hereward. "I think you're going to be pleasantly surprised."

"No doubt, no doubt." Hereward beamed at them all impartially. "There are always delightful surprises in store at Cosgreave Hall. The hospitality of this house is becoming legendary. As is—" he sketched a bow towards Dinah and Bunty—"the beauty of its ladies."

Leonora caught the glance that Phil and Eddie exchanged. As another American, she could interpret it freely and she smiled. Perhaps this evening was going to be more amusing than she had thought. In any case, she had been trapped into it, so she might as well relax and try to enjoy it.

What she would never enjoy was the other entrapment: she had been forced into a conspiracy. What was probably a criminal conspiracy. And the conspirators had the nerve to entertain the Chief Constable of the County in their own home just four days after the act.

Or . . . was Dear Hereward another conspirator? Tessa was his daughter, how far would he go to protect her from the consequences of her actions? If his daughter were to be convicted of reckless driving—no, *drunken* driving—vehicular manslaughter—the scandal would reflect on him.

Do you know who her father is? Eddie had demanded, ashen-faced. Would her father have to resign as Chief Constable if his daughter's crime was revealed? For that matter, what would be the repercussions for Bunty and Eddie? And Molly and Giles? They were all accessories after the fact.

And so was she now. One more conspirator, willing or not.

"Are you sure you're all right?"

"Oh!" She jumped. She had not noticed Annabel at her elbow. "Yes, yes, I'm fine. I was just . . . thinking."

"You should avoid deep thought if it makes you look like that. At least, don't think in public. Have pity on the rest of us. You looked decidedly odd there, for a moment. I thought you were going to have some sort of seizure."

"Sorry." Leonora smiled faintly. It was Annabel who would have had the seizure if she were a mind-reader. "I'll be more careful in future."

"Do—or you'll frighten the horses." Annabel studied her thoughtfully. "You know, if you ever have any little problems you might like to talk over . . ."

"Shall we go in to dinner now?" Lady Cosgreave interrupted loudly, giving Leonora no chance to weaken, even if she had felt like it. "No, not that way, James, we're using the small dining-room tonight. So much cosier when there are so few of us."

"The offer stands," Annabel muttered as they all moved towards the indicated room.

"Thank you," Leonora said, "but I don't really have any little problems." It was quite true.

All her problems were large ones.

Dinner proceeded smoothly until the final course. The two girls from the village served with more enthusiasm than skill, but made no serious mistakes. The vaunted wine was a bit too heavy for Leonora's taste but was the perfect accompaniment for the game-and-oyster pie, which was also a bit too heavy. Hereward was delighted with it, however, and it was increasingly clear that Hereward's opinion was the only one that mattered tonight.

In the course of desultory conversation, Leonora had learned that Hereward had been a widower for the past five years, that Tessa was his only daughter and that there was a son in a minor diplomatic post in an extremely sensitive part of the world.

It also became quite apparent that Hereward was not only a prime example of the aristocracy, but that he was also mega-rich. Lady Cosgreave and Bunty were close to fawning on him and Eddie was listening to his every word with exaggerated deference.

Annabel observed their behavior with barely-veiled cynicism. Hereward seemed to feel that it was no more than his due. Phil Mottram occasionally added to their conversation in a respectful tone, but James remained silent and ate his way stolidly through every course.

After the maid had cleared the dessert plates and deposited the port decanter at Eddie's elbow, Leonora was not at all surprised to see Bunty and her mother exchange glances and rise.

"Shall we leave the gentlemen to their port and cigars?" Lady Cosgreave suggested formally.

Hereward had already brought out a cigar, clipped off one end and was ritually bathing the other end in the flame of his lighter. James shied back from the naked flame, watching him with a horrified fascination.

"Perhaps we should invite James to come along with us." Annabel deftly threw a monkey-wrench into the well-ordered routine. "I don't think he cares much for port and cigars."

"Oh, yes—" James pushed back his chair, radiating relief.

"Sit down!" Eddie snapped.

James dropped back into his chair, looking trapped.

"I mean—" Eddie softened his command. "You want to stay here with us. If you don't want port, you can have something else. Phil's got some great new stories—you don't want to miss them."

"Er, no," James said weakly, slumping in his chair. "No . . ." He looked after the women wistfully as they left the room.

"Poor old James," Annabel said, closing the door behind them. "Eddie should have let him leave. He won't appreciate their smoking-room stories."

"I dare say they have other things to discuss as well," Lady Cosgreave said.

"Ah!" Annabel pursed her lips and glanced back at the closed door. "Poor old James."

"I can assure you your concern is quite misplaced," Lady Cosgreave said coldly. "James won't be *that* bored."

"More's the pity," Annabel said briskly.

"I thought we'd use the library tonight." Bunty sounded placating. "There are so few of us. And the drawing-room curtains haven't been replaced yet. It's still a bit of a mess in there."

"Very tactful," Annabel said. "When *are* you planning to start the redecoration?"

"Oh, soon . . ." Bunty opened the library door; a small cheery fire was burning in the grate, a drinks tray lurked at the back of the library table. At the front of the table, a coffee pot bubbled atop a small rack set over a flame burning low in its glass container. Cups and saucers were set out around it; a plate of mints and truffles and another of *petits fours* were temptingly placed beside them.

"Bit too tempting, don't you think?" Annabel echoed Leonora's thought, but there seemed to be an underlying meaning in her tone.

"*Do* sit down." Lady Cosgreave commandeered the wing chair beside the fire. "You *hover* so, Annabel."

"Armagnac!" Far from sitting down, Annabel had been prowling the room. Now she pounced on the drinks tray. "I could do with a splash of that. What about the rest of you?"

"I'll have a bit of the good old Tia Maria." Bunty settled herself in the armchair opposite her mother and stretched out her legs luxuriously. "You can do the honours, Annabel." She dispensed the permission Annabel had already taken for granted.

"Oh, the Grand Marnier, thank you, Annabel." Lady Cosgreave leaned back in her chair and closed her eyes, happily abdicating all responsibility.

"Here we are." Annabel dispensed the requested liqueurs. "What about you, Leonora?"

"Oh, er, anything." Leonora flinched, knowing the disapproval that would greet this indecisiveness. "I don't mind which."

"You *must* have a preference!" Annabel was stern. "Come now, what would you like?"

"Oh—" Leonora took the easy way out. "I'll have what you're having." That ought to be safe.

"Armagnac." Annabel was mollified. "Good choice. I *knew* you were just being shy," she said complacently. "Stands to reason, *everyone* really prefers their own brew. No point in fudging it. Always speak up—there's plenty here." She poured Armagnac into two glasses, carried them over to the three-seater Chesterfield sofa and, handing one to Leonora, sank down into the opposite corner of the sofa with her own.

"Ah, this is more like it." Annabel swirled the liquid around in her glass for a moment, then raised it on high. "Well, here's to crime!"

"I *beg* your pardon!" Bunty was offended.

"Really, Annabel!" Lady Cosgreave said. "You might have better taste."

"What's the matter?" Unaware of her hostesses' tender consciences, Annabel did not recognize the enormity of her gaffe.

Leonora sipped her Armagnac demurely, carefully avoiding eye contact with anyone at all.

"Olde English toast." Annabel was on the defensive. "Joke, really. You know."

"That's *so* like you, Annabel," Lady Cosgreave reproved. "You never did have any sense of the fitness of things."

"Don't be silly, Dinah," Annabel protested. "There's nobody here but us chickens. I shouldn't have dreamed of saying it if . . . if any of the people concerned were present."

That probably made matters worse, but Leonora did not raise her eyes to find out. The deep silence was too daunting.

"Oh, all right." Even Annabel was daunted. "I apologize, I suppose. But I do think you're making too much of a simple—"

"I s-say—" The door burst open and James stood in the doorway, pale and quivering. "B-Bunty, I think you'd better come at once!"

"What?" Both Bunty and Lady Cosgreave surged to their feet.

"It's Eddie." James stared at them wildly. "He—he's just collapsed. He looks terrible. Oh, hurry!"

CHAPTER 13

"Must've got a bad oyster." Hereward looked down at his host, sprawled upon the floor at his feet. "No warning. Just suddenly keeled over. Has to have been a bad oyster."

"Oh, don't say that!" Bunty cried, kneeling beside Eddie. "Mrs. Matthews will never cook for us again if she hears you."

"Eddie has been working too hard," Lady Cosgreave pronounced. "You really must make him take a holiday, Bunty."

As Eddie was a delicate shade of blue, Leonora considered that Lady Cosgreave was being extremely optimistic.

"Kiss of life, do you think?" Annabel was out of her depth, but game. "Anyone know how? Last time I took a First Aid course, it was a question of rolling them over on their tums, straddling them, and proceeding with the old *One-and-two* and *One-and-Two* . . ."

"I've called the doctor," James said, coming back into the room. "That is, he wasn't there, but the locum is coming."

"Oh, good show!" Hereward approved. "Should we loosen any clothing, do you think? Or does that just apply to ladies' stays?" It sounded as though his last First Aid course had pre-dated even Annabel's.

"Help me to get him upstairs—" Bunty tugged at Eddie's arm, moving him only slightly. "Into bed. He'll be better there."

"An emetic!" Lady Cosgreave said decisively. "Get him into the bathroom. Annabel, mix up some salt, mustard, vinegar—"

"Good God!" Annabel was appalled. "I should think that would kill him faster than anything."

"Oh, don't just stand there arguing—" Bunty wailed. "Help me!"

"The doctor's coming," James said. "I told him it was urgent. He'll be here any moment."

"Eddie!" Bunty tugged at her husband's arm. "Eddie, can you hear me? Eddie, wake up!"

"Take it easy." Phil Mottram crouched beside her and gently wrestled Eddie's arm away from her. Which was just as well, Leonora thought. Bunty had been clutching it tightly enough to cut off his circulation.

"Easy, now." Phil clamped Eddie's wrist, settled his two middle fingers over the pulse region, and looked thoughtful.

"How is he?" Leonora asked softly.

Phil shot her an annoyed warning glance and she realized abruptly that he had no more idea than she had. He was faking competence in an attempt to steady Bunty.

"Maybe we ought to get him to bed," Phil said. "How about you guys lending a hand?"

Hereward and James looked equally startled at being so addressed, but recovered quickly and came forward. Phil took the precautions of loosening Eddie's necktie and belt, then they worked together to lift and carry him.

"Upstairs—" Bunty directed.

"I think maybe we ought to keep him down here." Phil, obviously having second thoughts, divided a dubious glance between the flight of stairs and his two helpers. "Just until the doctor sees him. Then we'll know whether he might be better off going to the nearest hospital instead."

"But I want him to be comfortable—"

"I don't believe he's actually noticing." James, too, did not relish trying to wrestle Eddie up the staircase.

"Much better to keep him down here, m'dear." Neither did Hereward wish to risk a hernia.

"Easy around the corner, fellas." Phil, supporting Eddie's head and shoulders, began negotiating the turn at the doorway.

Eddie opened one eye and muttered something, twitching feebly.

"What did he say?" Bunty pushed past Phil to get at her husband. "Eddie! Eddie, darling. Speak to me!"

The doorbell shrilled abruptly, startling them all and almost causing James to drop Eddie's left leg. Hereward kept a stalwart grip on the right leg.

"I'll go!" Annabel darted for the door. "It must be the quack."

The small procession with Eddie at the center continued on its way. Bunty led them into the main drawing-room, perhaps because the sofa in the smaller, warmer library was not large enough to accommodate Eddie's ample bulk.

"Here we are!" Annabel reappeared with a small thin man in her wake. "It *is* the—uh, doctor."

"Good, good." Hereward had decided to take command, as Bunty had thrown herself on her knees at her husband's side, oblivious of everything else. Lady Cosgreave was roaming round the room, snapping on lamps—except for the one which would illuminate the fire damage.

"Right over here, doctor," Hereward said.

The doctor, who had already deduced that for himself, gave Bunty an impatient look as he tried to take her place at Eddie's side.

"He's better!" Bunty clutched at the doctor's arm, impeding him. "He's better already, isn't he? His color's coming back."

Eddie was mumbling now; he did look slightly improved. The doctor shook off Bunty's hand and bent over him.

"Did you bring along your stomach pump?" Hereward moved in and leaned over the doctor's shoulder, nearly knocking him off balance. "Get rid of that oyster, that's what he needs—" He freely gave a second opinion. "I remember one time in—"

"Yes, quite." The doctor straightened up abruptly, sending Hereward staggering backwards. "I think it might be best if we cleared the room. I'd like to examine the patient privately."

"Oh, but not *me*," Bunty protested. "I'm his *wife*."

That, the doctor's look told her, *was part of the problem*. "Just for a few minutes," he promised unconvincingly.

"Come on, honey." Phil's arm circled Bunty's waist, urging her from the room. She struggled against him, looking back over her shoulder.

"Be brave, m'dear," Hereward advised. "Eddie's in the best of hands . . . I'm sure." He led the others into the reception hall.

"Eddie has been working much too hard," Lady Cosgreave said, not disapprovingly. "And the stock market has been so erratic. It's not surprising that he should be feeling the strain."

"That's right," Hereward said. "The doctor will fix him up. Probably just needs a tonic."

"Sure, that's all it is." Phil agreed, a little too hastily. "Overwork. He needs a good rest. Maybe the two of you ought to take a little trip somewhere. A cruise, or something."

"That's not a bad idea." Lady Cosgreave was suddenly thoughtful. "It might be best to get away for a while . . . escape the winter. Follow the sun . . ."

Get away was the operative phrase. Leonora could see it all unrolling before her. Bunty and Eddie now had a perfect excuse to leave the country for an indeterminate length of time, during which Horton's body could be discovered in circumstances that had nothing to do with them. Had Eddie's collapse been deliberately staged?

"In fact," Lady Cosgreave decided, "I might go along, too. I could do with a holiday."

Then they'd all be out of the country. Leonora wondered if Molly and Giles were also preparing their escape route. Soon there wouldn't be anyone left around here who knew what the original situation had been. Except herself. Perhaps she ought to be planning to leave while there was still time. Was that what Lady Cosgreave's delicate frown was trying to signal to her?

"I really think—" she began.

The drawing-room door opened and no one was paying any attention to her any more. They all turned towards the door and waited for some pronouncement from the doctor, who was standing in the doorway, regarding them all with disfavor.

"How is he?" Bunty started forward. "Can I go in now?"

"He's come round." The doctor blocked her way. "Basically, he's all right, I think, but I'd like to run a few tests. I'll need to get him to hospital for that—"

"Hospital!" Bunty was horrified. "Tonight?"

"Tonight," the doctor said firmly. "The sooner the better." It was clear that he thought the atmosphere too disruptive for an ailing man.

"Called an ambulance, have you?" Hereward asked.

"I don't think that's necessary. I'll drive him in my car." The doctor looked at Bunty. "You might pack an overnight case for him. Just a few necessities."

"Yes, yes, of course." Bunty whirled and headed for the stairs.

Leonora found that she, Annabel and James had instinctively drawn together into a tight little group of their own: the outsiders in this family emergency.

Lady Cosgreave and Hereward were now conversing quietly with the doctor. Phil Mottram hovered irresolutely between the two groups, uncertain of his status.

"Maybe—" he looked from one group to the other unhappily—"maybe I ought to go upstairs and see if I can help Bunty."

No one appeared to pay any attention to the suggestion and, after a moment, he edged towards the staircase and disappeared.

"Rather a nice chap," Hereward said to Lady Cosgreave, as soon as Phil was out of earshot. "I'm pleased to have had the opportunity to meet him. I gather he's a very good friend of Tessa's, but Lord knows when she'll get around to introducing us. Just before the ceremony, probably." He sighed heavily. "I don't know . . . young people these days!"

"Not the way it was in our salad days," Lady Cosgreave agreed. "Still, you've had the chance to look him over and that's the important thing. It's so nice to be able to put a face to the name when the children begin to prattle about their friends."

Annabel barely repressed a snort. It was clear that she could not visualize either Bunty or Tessa as prattling types. She gave a cynical glance towards the staircase and then looked at James. He was looking at his watch.

"Er, um," he suggested. "D'you think it might be a good idea if we left them to it? We aren't of any use and, um, I'd say the party's over."

"Good point, James." Annabel nodded. "I would agree that the party is definitely over. Time for us to move along."

"Oh yes!" Leonora felt a surge of enthusiasm. "We should have thought of it earlier."

"We couldn't have done it earlier," Annabel said. "Not before the quack arrived."

"But it's quite in order now." James moved forward with more firmness than he had yet shown, heading for Lady Cosgreave.

"We might as well." Annabel followed him. "Bunty may be some time."

Leonora wasn't going to argue. The prospect of ending the evening was like an oasis shimmering in the distance. She just wanted to get away before anything else happened.

Where had that thought come from? What else did she think might happen?

In this house, practically anything. She had never yet had a peaceful meal in it.

Hoping her thought didn't show in her face, she echoed Annabel's goodbye to their substitute hostess. They hadn't quite gained the door, however, when Bunty came down the staircase and they had to pause and reiterate their farewells to their proper hostess.

"Oh, must you go?" Bunty's response was automatic and devoid of any genuine regret, or even interest.

"Yes, oh yes," James blurted out. "You don't want us underfoot at a time like this. We must leave you to your sorr— Er, we must leave. Goodbye."

"You'll stay, Hereward," Lady Cosgreave commanded.

"Certainly. Might be something I can do."

"You're such a comfort to me." Lady Cosgreave patted his arm.

"Party breaking up?" Phil appeared at the foot of the stairs, carrying Eddie's overnight case. "Yeah," he answered himself. "I guess it was time we were all leaving."

"Not you, Phil," Bunty said quickly. She added. "The doctor will need help getting Eddie out to the car and you're—" As though suddenly aware of tactlessness, she broke off.

He was younger, stronger, fitter than any of the other men. Better able to bear the burden. They recognized this, although James flushed and looked miserable.

"Okay." Phil set down the case. "I'll go and see if he's ready for me now." He went into the drawing-room and there was a low murmur of voices.

Annabel started firmly for the front door. "No use hanging about," she said to James and Leonora. "If 'twere done when 'tis done, 'twere well it were done quickly."

"You shouldn't quote from that play." It seemed to add to James's misery. "Bad luck."

"Nonsense!" Annabel said. "That's theatrical superstition—we have nothing to do with the theater."

"The senior boys put it on at school once," James said. "That term we had three broken legs, a dislocated shoulder and an attempted suicide. We never put it on again."

Lady Cosgreave looked at them as though the quotation trembling on *her* lips was, "Stand not upon the order of your going—but go at once!"

"Sheer coincidence!" Annabel opened the door and sketched a wave to Lady Cosgreave.

Then Phil and the doctor emerged from the drawing-room supporting Eddie between them. Eddie's face had lost its blueish tinge, but was pale and drawn; he seemed half-conscious, but he was trying to walk. Bunty picked up his suitcase and followed the trio.

Annabel darted forward to open the door of the doctor's car. Then there was a further delay while everyone settled Eddie in the back seat with Bunty beside him.

"You *will* stay—" Bunty clung to Phil's hand. "Wait for me. I'll be back after we get Eddie comfortable—" There were tears in her eyes, her hair was disarrayed. There was also something about Phil's rumpled lapels that suggested tears had already been shed on them.

"I'll wait." He patted her hand awkwardly, smiling reassurance over her head to Eddie, who seemed to be using the last of his strength to sit upright.

Car doors slammed, Phil stepped back. Lady Cosgreave and Hereward waved. The car moved off down the driveway.

"Come on." Annabel rallied her own troops. "Let's go back to my place and have coffee."

Leonora followed willingly, but James balked, still staring after the car.

"It's probably a coronary." He was plunged in gloom. "Poor old chap has been working so hard, all those worries with the financial market going mad. The fire was probably the last straw—'' He broke off.

''More likely exhausted trying to keep up with the dance Bunty leads him.'' Annabel said. ''Come and have some coffee.''

''No, thank you.'' James turned away. ''I think I've had enough for tonight. Quite enough. I just want to go home.''

''You'll come?'' Annabel looked at Leonora.

''If you're sure it won't be too much trouble—''

''None at all,'' Annabel said. ''I think we need to wind down after the excitement. Sure you won't change your mind, James?''

But James had already left them.

CHAPTER 14

"Pity about James. Too nervy by half. Wish there were something more we could do about it." Annabel refilled the coffee cups and also the brandy glasses. Who said she never drank anything but martinis?

"He does seem very high-strung," Leonora said.

"Legacy of thirty years of trying to ram some knowledge into thick young heads. Wonder more of them don't crack up."

"Perhaps they do, but no one ever notices it because they're so eccentric to begin with." Leonora was willing to follow this train of thought. It could lead-in to some of the questions she wanted to ask. "I had a couple of teachers like that."

"Hadn't we all!" Annabel snorted. "Half the teachers at my girlhood school would have been interchangeable with the occupants of any reasonably-appointed looney-bin." She grew thoughtful. "Not that things are so very different now."

"Do you think Eddie is cracking up?"

"It's a more likely theory than that of a bad oyster, isn't it? Particularly as we all had some of the oysters in that game pie. If one were that bad, the taint would have spread through in the cooking, I should think, and the rest of us would be feeling at least a little queasy by now. But I feel fine, don't you?"

"Just fine," Leonora agreed absently. "And everyone else seemed to be all right. It couldn't have been the food."

"If it had been, Hereward should have been the first to keel over," Annabel said. "Did you notice? He was filching the oysters from Dinah's plate? She doesn't like them and she'd pushed them to one side and he—greedy-guts—helped himself to them."

"As a matter of fact, I had noticed. I was a bit surprised."

"Dinah was encouraging him, of course. Perhaps she thought they'd do something for him." Annabel snorted. "If she has any expectations in that direction, she'd better hurry things along. After the Andrews family realize the state of play, Dinah might not be considered a suitable stepmamma for Tessa—and Bunty certainly wouldn't be welcome as a stepsister."

"Oh!" And yet Leonora was not really surprised that Annabel knew. It had been over-optimistic to assume that she would have walked out of that suspicious gathering the other day and not done her best to find out what had been going on. "Yes, and I suppose it would be especially embarrassing because of him being Chief Constable. At best, it might look as though they were making a fool of him."

"Mmmm-hmmmm . . ." Annabel gave her an oblique look and tipped another splash of brandy into her glass. "Exactly. And . . . at worst?"

"Well, I suppose it would be simply awful for him to have to arrest his friends."

"Simply awful!" Annabel said with muted glee.

"Not to mention his daughter." Leonora began to have the uneasy feeling that she was talking too much. Annabel's eyes had begun to gleam more brightly than her diamonds and she looked to be on the verge of purring.

"Oh, *do* let's mention his daughter!" She *was* purring. "What about Tessa?"

"Oh, nothing, really." Leonora set down her glass casually. "I'm talking too much—and I don't even know what I'm talking about." She reached for her coffee cup and took a large swallow, discovering too late that Annabel must have poured a generous dollop of brandy into it when she wasn't watching.

"Such a sweet gel, Tessa," Annabel prompted. "Much too nice to be able to deal with the harsher complexities of life, I've always thought."

"She needn't worry." Leonora was conscious that bitterness was winning out over discretion. "There seem to be enough people around who are willing to shield her from them."

"Do you think so?" Annabel honestly wanted to know. "I'd have said she wasn't aware of most of them."

"That's right." Leonora was confused. Perhaps Annabel *did* know all about it. "I think it happened without her knowing—just a glancing blow when she swerved. She was probably so busy trying to avoid the animal that she never even saw him."

"She hit someone!" Annabel pounced. "Who?"

"Don't you know?"

"I can guess." It was a transparent lie. Annabel hadn't a clue—except for the ones Leonora had just given her. "But tell me, anyway."

"No—No—" Leonora started to rise. "I think I ought to go now—"

"Not yet." Annabel pushed her back into her chair and thrust the glass into her hand. "You were going to tell me all about it—remember? Not that I don't know most of it," she bluffed. "But I'm still hazy on some of the details. Come on now," she coaxed. "Tell Annabel all about it."

Well, why not? She hadn't been able to talk it over with anyone else. Everyone up at Cosgreave Hall was pretending it hadn't happened. Or that, if it had, it was somehow her fault. At least Annabel was willing to listen. Eager, in fact.

"I don't know . . ." Where did she begin? How much had Annabel already pieced together? "Suppose *you* tell *me*—" she decided to approach it obliquely. "The man who used to have my cottage . . . the ex-gardener. Horton?"

"You know about that, do you?" Annabel was not surprised. "Or have you been having trouble with him, too? He's been making a nuisance of himself again, has he?"

"Those footsteps outside . . ." Leonora said vaguely. "They must have been his."

"Just like the silly old fool," Annabel said. "They should have got rid of him long ago. He's been nothing but trouble ever since I've been living here—and long before that, unless I miss my guess. Nasty, vindictive type—and a rotten gardener. They're much better off without him."

Something in Leonora's face must have given her away. Annabel watched her expression change and whistled soundlessly.

"You mean it's Horton? He's the one she hit?"

"What I don't understand," Leonora said, "is how long they think they can conceal it. Won't people notice he's absent from his usual haunts? Won't someone come looking for him? Hasn't he friends? A family? Won't anyone miss him?"

"Not very much," Annabel said. "He was an unpleasant surly type. There were two daughters—one's in Canada, the other's in Australia, and a son in the Merchant Navy. I shouldn't think any of them were much at letter-writing."

"Then it might take a couple of years of missing Christmas cards before the family noticed." It was becoming clearer to Leonora now. The longer the delaying action was successful, the less chance there would be of anyone discovering what had really happened to Horton.

"Now tell me—" Annabel dropped all pretence that she already knew what they were talking about. "Tell me the rest of it. You might as well, you've gone this far. Who knows, perhaps I might be able to help.'' She studied Leonora shrewdly. ''You do look as though you needed help, you know.''

Why not? The sheer relief of confiding in someone who believed her would be help enough. It was a bonus that Annabel, unlike the others, was not going to try to persuade her that she had never seen what she knew she had seen; or, failing that, resort to veiled threats to convince her that she ought to join in the conspiracy of silence.

''Come on.'' Annabel did not hold with silence at all. ''Tell me. Why will the family have to wait several years before they realize Horton is dead? He *is* dead, isn't he? And what was all that about concealing it?''

''They've hidden the body,'' Leonora blurted out. ''They've taken it out from under the bush and hidden it. I don't know where. And Lady Cosgreave says I can never prove anything without a *corpus delicti*—and, if I try, the police will only think I'm a liar and a troublemaker because I'm a foreigner and . . . and . . .'' She was trying not to cry. It would be too embarrassing.

''Dinah is quite mistaken,'' Annabel said. ''She often is, and one notices that the mistakes are always in her own favor. *Corpus delicti* does not mean the *body*, it refers to the body of the crime. If you can give evidence that a crime has been committed, then that is the *corpus delicti* from which the police can begin their investigation.'' She added thoughtfully, ''I can see that Dinah has been trying to intimidate you. She's rather good at that.''

''She *did* intimidate me.'' Leonora was annoyed to hear herself give a pathetic little sniffle; tears were still too close for comfort. ''When she said that they'd be able to prove I was a liar and maybe mentally unbalanced—'' Another sniffle escaped.

''Just carry on, you're doing fine. Don't stop now. Have a bit more brandy—'' In the act of pouring, Annabel hesitated. ''Or would you rather switch to martinis?''

"No, no! I mean, no, thank you." The enormity of the suggestion brought Leonora out of her little bout of self-pity; self-preservation took precedence.

"As you please." Annabel sounded disappointed, evidently feeling that she could not make the switch herself if her guest did not. "Go on. What was that bit about proving you were a liar and mentally unbalanced?"

"I'm not. Honestly, I'm not. And it's all Lady Cosgreave's fault, anyway. She told me to lie in the first place because—" Leonora broke off abruptly, remembering too late that she had been advised to lie in order to escape Annabel's inquisitions. Now she was right in the middle of one.

"And Molly is lying, too." Ruthlessly, she threw the Carmodys to the wolves. "And Giles helped Eddie dispose of the body. And Lady Cosgreave says they'll both deny everything."

"They undoubtedly will. They're very good at covering their tracks. They've had to be." Annabel nodded decisively. "But tell me how they got into this."

"Molly said the man was dead. I saw the foot sticking out from under the bush, but she went in and looked. I didn't. I wish I had. Now Lady Cosgreave says the man wasn't dead at all and he must have got up and walked away. But Molly definitely said that he was dead. I asked her if she was sure and she said she'd been a nurse before she married Giles, so she knew, and there was nothing we could do for the man."

"I don't think she said that." Annabel shook her head.

"She did. He *was* dead. Don't tell me you're going to be like Lady Cosgreave and try to convince me it was all a mistake."

"Never!" Annabel shuddered. "Dinah and I are poles apart. I mean that Molly could never have told you that she was a nurse before she married Giles."

"You mean she wasn't?"

"No, I mean . . . Well," Annabel's eyes glinted with mischief. "Put it this way: Molly and Giles have been married for thirty years—but not to each other."

"What?"

"So, you see, she couldn't have said she was a nurse before she married Giles. She was a nurse, all right, but it was before she married her real husband."

"Oh. Maybe she said it was before she met Giles—and I just assumed she meant before she married him."

"That must be it."

"Then that's why Molly and Giles do what Eddie and Bunty want them to do. Molly said I shouldn't call the police until she'd told Eddie and Bunty; then they came down with Giles and—"

"And that was what I walked in on. I knew there was something going on," Annabel said with satisfaction. "I didn't know what, but I promised myself I'd find out."

Leonora remembered that there were a few more things she wanted to find out herself. "What could they have done with the body? They must have moved it that night. They'd been talking about taking it away and leaving it down by the pub—because they insisted he must have been injured in a fight there. But if they'd done that, he'd have been found by now."

"Probably had second thoughts." Annabel leaned back and gazed into the amber depths of her glass. "There's a strong current in the river, they could have slid him in and hoped he'd be carried out to sea. Or else that he'd surface far enough downstream to be unidentified. Then there are caves and pot-holes around this region, drop him down one and it could be years before weekend explorers discovered the skeleton. Or," she finished cheerfully, "they might simply have buried him somewhere."

"You mean—" Leonora faced the fact slowly—"we may never find out where he is. Unless one of them tells us."

"I wouldn't put much money on that," Annabel said.

"After going to all this trouble to hide the body, they aren't likely to have a crisis of conscience and blurt out a confession."

"No—" Leonora thought of the solid front presented by Eddie, his wife and mother-in-law—and even his tenants. "No, I guess not."

"There you are, then." Annabel shrugged and gazed off into space. "They've covered their tracks—"

"Tessa's tracks," Leonora said.

"Ah yes." Annabel accepted the correction. "And Tessa had been drinking, hadn't she? Hard lines, to have driven all the way down from Town and then had an accident on the doorstep. One can see their point. There'd be a prosecution, she'd lose her license, probably a heavy fine, if not worse. And then there'd always be people who felt Eddie should never have let such a thing happen to a guest of his. They'd have felt he should have done something to protect her from the consequences—"

"Which he did do," Leonora pointed out. "Thereby ingratiating himself with his wealthy and aristocratic City colleagues. Only—" There was a flaw in this argument. "Only they wouldn't know he'd protected Tessa, because no one knew Horton had been hit. Even Tessa might not have known it. She bumped her own head when she hit the gatepost. And she'd been trying to avoid an animal running across her path. She might not have seen Horton at all."

"For that matter," Annabel said slowly, "neither did we. And we were on the scene almost as soon as the accident happened."

"There was so much confusion," Leonora reminded her. "Everyone was shouting. We couldn't have heard someone groaning faintly."

"There *is* that," Annabel admitted. "And yet . . ."

"Oh, what does it matter?" A wave of despair swept over

Leonora. "Why are we even discussing it? When it comes down to it, there's no proof at all. It would be my word against theirs—and there are so many of them."

"Ah, but you have *me* on your side now." Annabel topped up their glasses. "I believe you."

"Thanks." The vote of confidence was not the comfort it might have been. If Lady Cosgreave and her cohorts were prepared to smear Leonora as a mentally disturbed liar, what might they not do with Annabel's capacity for gossip, not to mention her martini intake? Leonora felt that she could have done with a more plausible ally.

"You know," Annabel said, "it's been years since I've tried my hand at sketching, but I think I'll hunt out that old charcoal and sketchpad and go out sketching with you tomorrow. It will give us an excuse to cover a lot of territory. Who knows what we might find?"

CHAPTER 15

The morning was grey, although it was not actually raining. Perhaps the day would improve, it was still terribly early. When Annabel had insisted on an early start, Leonora had had no idea she meant *this* early. At least, it ought to ensure that no one at Cosgreave Hall would witness their departure.

Annabel's sketchpad was so old that it bore the trade mark of a firm long out of business; her charcoal stick was an odd shape and looked suspiciously like something filched from a coal scuttle. She had chosen to array herself in a decrepit tweed skirt and twin set, covered by a voluminous smock which might have begun life as a maternity garment. Either she considered her diamond rings *de rigueur* for every occasion, or she had worn them for so long that she was no longer able to remove them.

"We'll start in the most obvious place," she announced to Leonora. "His cottage. The one he moved to after being turned out of your place. It's on the far side of the river. That would be the logical place for him to be found dead. Perhaps lying at the foot of the stairs to account for the head injuries." She struck off across the lawn without a backward glance.

Leonora followed slowly, feeling resentful. Annabel was enjoying this. It was a game to her, even though she knew the people involved a lot better than Leonora did. Perhaps she did not like them very much and felt that they deserved to have their schemes overturned.

Or perhaps the thrill of the chase was going to her head. Annabel paused at the slope leading down to the river and motioned Leonora forward impatiently.

"We'll walk along the towpath to the bridge." Annabel said it too casually. Leonora was not surprised when she added, even more casually, "We can keep an eye on the river as we go. Doubt that we'll see anything—otherwise someone would have discovered it before this—but it won't hurt to look."

"All right." The day suddenly seemed more threatening. Leonora looked out over the rippling water. In the distance, on the other side of the river, a small van was driving purposefully towards the bridge. Another delivery for Clio? With a pang, Leonora realized how much her New York friends would envy her for living, even temporarily, in such beautiful surroundings in a place where olde worlde service still existed. To an outsider, even this stroll along the towpath with a friend would look idyllic—if they did not know the grim purpose behind it.

"Hold on!" Annabel picked up a stick and advanced to the river's edge where she poked at something in the shallows. After a moment, an empty discarded crisp packet rose on the end of her stick.

"False alarm." She shook the brightly colored wrapper off her stick. "For a moment, I thought—"

She did not finish the sentence and Leonora did not ask what she had thought. They continued strolling along the river bank, Annabel still carrying the stick and looking for another opportunity to use it.

Just as they reached the bridge, the van passed them.

"Good heavens," Leonora said. "Even the ironmonger delivers in this country."

"Only to Clio," Annabel said drily.

"Clio," Leonora sighed. "What it is to be irresistible."

"Only to tradesmen." Annabel's tone was even drier and Leonora remembered that Clio's husband seemed to spend an inordinate amount of time away from home.

"I haven't met Clio's husband yet," she said. "Wasn't he due back from his business trip by now?"

"Tom never hurries," Annabel said. "Unless he's on his way to do business. He always takes his time about coming back. One can't blame Clio for—" She broke off.

"Yes?" Leonora prompted, but Annabel seemed to have thought better of her intended remark. She shrugged and lengthened her steps.

"Not far now," she said, once they had crossed the bridge. "We turn down here." She led the way along a narrow road running parallel with the river and flanked at intervals by cottages and dilapidated bungalows in various stages of disintegration.

"Prefab housing," Annabel identified. "They called it an emergency measure when they began rebuilding just after the war. They were only intended to be temporary—it's a wonder some of them are still standing."

"Some of them look quite nice." Leonora noticed the well-tended gardens in front and fresh paintwork on the buildings.

"These aren't bad," Annabel admitted. "They're pretty well kept up in this section. Horton's cottage isn't, of course, not even the garden. Least of all," she corrected herself, "the garden. Have you ever noticed that professional gardeners have the worst-kept gardens? They expend all their energies on other people's gardens and just want to sit back and watch the weeds grow when they're at home. That's his place, just ahead."

It was the last house in the lane, and the shabbiest, standing well back from the road and surrounded by a tangle of shrubbery. It looked as though it might have been one of the original dwellings on the road.

"You can see why he preferred the cottage on the estate, can't you?" Annabel led the way down the overgrown path.

The paint on the woodwork was peeling and it had been a long time since the grimy curtains behind the windows had seen better days.

"Just for form's sake—" Annabel marched up to the door and rang the bell. No one answered. She rang again, then tried the door. It was locked.

"Now what?" Leonora asked.

"You stay here. I'll take a look round the back." Annabel slipped through a gap in the bushes and disappeared.

After a short silence, the sound of breaking glass confirmed Leonora's worst suspicions.

"Annabel?" she called. "Annabel, is everything all right?"

Silence answered her. Even the birds seemed to have stopped singing and all the country noises had ceased.

"Annabel?" She started forward, looking for the spot where Annabel had disappeared into the shrubbery.

"Here we are." The door opened behind her. "Hurry up," Annabel said. "Don't stand about. We don't want to make ourselves conspicuous. You never know who might be watching."

"You broke in," Leonora said incredulously.

"Don't dither on the doorstep!" Annabel grasped her arm and yanked her inside, slamming the door behind her.

"This is breaking and entering." Leonora resisted a strong impulse to wring her hands.

"Nonsense!" Annabel said. "I was walking past when I noticed a broken window, so I came in to see if everything was all right. The police do it all the time—and in just that way."

"But we're not the police."

"No," Annabel said regretfully. "But—" she brightened—"we're helping them with their inquiries."

"They don't know that."

"With any luck, they won't find out. Now stop wasting time and let's search the house."

"We're inside now, I suppose we might as well," Leonora agreed half-heartedly and followed in Annabel's wake as she charged through the house. Her first impression—that Annabel knew what she was doing—receded rapidly as Annabel rushed aimlessly around the drab, sparsely-furnished rooms, peering into every corner, stooping to look under the furniture and prodding at the back of closets with the stick she still carried.

"What are we looking for?" Leonora finally dared to ask.

"Clues."

"Will we know them if we find them?"

"Not much faith in me, have you?" Annabel straightened up and backed out of the corner she had been investigating.

"In anyone," Leonora said, recognizing the truth of her statement. "Not even myself." Again, she realized the damage Paul had done to her self-confidence.

"And you an artist," Annabel reprimanded absently. Although her attention was already centered on an as-yet unexplored corner of the sitting-room, Leonora felt that her incautious remark had been mentally filed for future reference.

"Nothing here." Annabel abandoned a pile of fluffy dust. "Let's try upstairs."

There was an old-fashioned bathroom at the top of the stairs. It had obviously been a second bedroom at one time and the grubby washbasin, toilet and bath looked lost in the midst of too much space. Nothing else there, except the ever-present dirt.

The next room was the bedroom. Annabel halted in the doorway with a sharp intake of breath. This room looked as though someone had just left it. There was the indentation of a body on top of the bedspread and a smear of dirt where the feet could have rested. A hint of tobacco smoke still seemed to hang in the air.

Uneasily, they moved forward, Annabel to stare down at the bed, Leonora to look at the ashtray on the bedside table. It was full of clues—overflowing, in fact. Stubs of English, American and French cigarettes of varying brands were piled high.

"What kind of cigarettes did Horton smoke?" she asked.

"Mostly OP's," Annabel said absently. Glancing up and noting Leonora's puzzled look, she translated. "Other people's. He seldom carried any of his own and, if anyone was rash enough to offer him their packet, he always took an extra one and tucked it away in his pocket to have at home later."

"That explains the ashtray."

"Oh yes." Annabel glanced at it. "That looks just about right. Typical of him. Must've been doing well with his cadging lately."

"I guess he was." Leonora twisted her head, trying to read the pale lettering on some of the stubs. "Some of these seem to be Arabic or Greek."

"Horton wasn't fussy, so long as they were free." Annabel bent over the bed and poked gingerly at the dark smear on the bedspread, then looked around.

"Leonora—don't move!" She straightened up and stared at the floor beside the bed.

"Why?" Leonora was instantly alarmed, visualizing something deadly slithering out from under the bed—or already coiled to strike at the slightest movement. She looked down at the floor but could see nothing.

"Don't move," Annabel warned again. "You'll tread on it and we'll lose it." She crouched to examine something close by Leonora's feet.

"What is it?" Leonora could not discern the dark blob that was interesting Annabel.

"Mud." Annabel tested it carefully with one finger. "Damp mud. Fresh mud. When did you say you found the body?"

"Why, uh, Saturday."

"So it would have dried out by now if it had been lying here since then. The mud on the bedspread seems fresh, too."

They looked at each other, neither willing to voice the thought in both their minds.

"Come on." Annabel started forward. "Let's finish searching the house."

There was not much more to see. Only one more room on that floor, a tiny one being used as storage space into which was crammed such a jumble of junk even Annabel paled.

"There can't be anything in there. No room for a body." She closed the door again hastily and moved away. 'Let's go back downstairs."

"There's just the kitchen left." Back on the ground floor, Leonora looked into the final room. It was, surprisingly, much tidier than the others. She would not have been surprised to see the table cluttered with the remains of Horton's last few meals, but all the crockery and silverware had been cleared away and the table was bare.

"Not much here." Annabel seemed disappointed.

"It's awfully clean." Leonora voiced her doubts. "Compared to the other rooms, I mean." It still could not be considered spotless.

"Oh, Horton *did* keep his kitchen—he called it his galley—clean, I'll give him that. He was in the Navy and that bit of training stuck. He kept the kitchen shipshape."

Once again, they met each other's eyes uneasily. Leonora looked over her shoulder at the door. Annabel prowled the room, still hunting clues.

"Strange—" She paused at the sink. "I wouldn't have expected to find any water in the sink." She checked. "And the tap's not dripping, either."

Leonora looked over her shoulder again. She was beginning to fear that someone—Horton?—might walk in on them at any moment.

"And—" Annabel had checked further—"the dish towel is still damp. What do you think of that?"

"I think we'd better get out of here."

"You may be right." Annabel took a final look around the room, shaking her head.

"You know," she said. "I wish you had taken a good look at that body yourself."

"So do I," Leonora said. "But it wouldn't have made a great deal of difference, would it? I'd never seen Horton before."

"So you hadn't," Annabel said thoughtfully. "You'd still have had to rely on Molly's identification."

Something in the house creaked alarmingly. They froze. After a long moment, Annabel gave a nervous laugh.

"Place is ready to fall down. It's a wonder it's stayed up this long."

A cold draught curled through the room, probably from the window Annabel had broken. Probably.

"Let's get out of here!" Leonora did not wait to see if Annabel was following her.

CHAPTER 16

When they got back to their own side of the river, Leonora was so unnerved that she found herself actually welcoming Annabel's suggestion of a martini break.

"Molly . . ." Annabel said thoughtfully, pouring the lethal mixture from a large pitcher. "Molly Carmody . . ."

"And don't forget Giles," Leonora said. "He was the one who helped Eddie take the body away. And now they're denying everything. Do you think, if we tackled them together . . . ?"

"No-o-o." Annabel became even more thoughtful. "I don't think it would do the slightest bit of good for us to tackle them, either singly or together. But you've just reminded me of something." She appeared to go off into deep thought.

"Yes?" Leonora prompted.

"Do you realize how remiss we've been?" Annabel asked accusingly. "Eddie—our dear host—was taken off to hospital last night and we haven't even inquired about him. That's shocking! We ought to find out how he is."

"Oh, heavens!" Leonora was conscience-stricken. It was not that she was indifferent to Eddie's fate, it was just that things had a way of getting sidetracked when Annabel was around.

"Should we go up to the Hall after our drink and ask after him?"

"Disturb Dinah and Bunty?" Annabel shuddered and finished her drink all in one motion. "Shouldn't dream of it! No, I'll ring the hospital and see how he's getting on. And—" her smile was too innocent to be true, as she poured fresh drinks— "and see if he's allowed visitors."

"He may be back home by now. He seemed to have been improving by the time the doctor got him into the car. The hospital might have released him this morning."

"If so, they'll tell us, but I doubt it. When a previously healthy man collapses like that, they want to get to the bottom of it. That takes time. He'll be there for a couple more days yet—and the sooner we get in to see him, the better."

"Do you really think he'll tell us anything?"

"I think he's the weakest link. Especially now. He'll have had too much time to think, lying there alone, feeling sorry for himself and without his precious computer and all his support systems. He'll be ready to welcome visitors and have a good talk."

"He might not want to talk about what we have in mind."

"We'll see. Finish your drink while I telephone."

It was worth trying, Leonora decided, absent-mindedly finishing her drink as Annabel had directed. Eddie, feeling vulnerable and insecure—as he must—and without his wife and mother-in-law to prompt him, might be more amenable to questioning than he had been so far. Especially if Annabel did a little judicious browbeating.

"He's there," Annabel reported, coming back into the room. "And he can have visitors. I'll just—" she glanced down at her sketching outfit. "I'll just change into something more suitable and we can go along."

"I'd like to change, too." Leonora stood up and tried to persuade herself that she had not swayed. "And maybe we could stop and get something to eat along the way."

"Oh, do you want to?" Annabel seemed vaguely surprised.

"Yes, I do," Leonora said firmly. "Very much." She started for the door and was relieved to find that she was fairly steady. Perhaps there would be time for a quick cup of coffee before Annabel was ready.

"I'll pick you up," Annabel said. "About half an hour."

For the first time, Leonora began to feel dissatisfied with her wardrobe. There was not very much choice. She settled for a blue-grey outfit and decided that she ought to invest in the local uniform. With winter coming on, some heavy wool skirts and twinsets were obviously indicated. Next time Clio offered, she would agree to a shopping expedition. Whether she remained in the cottage or not, it was already apparent that this climate required warmer clothing than she possessed.

The doorbell startled her. She glanced at her watch. Surely, Annabel could not have changed and got here so soon. The doorbell rang again—a long, imperative ring. Something urgent. Another emergency?

She hurried downstairs, still buttoning her skirt and paused to study the shadow on the other side of the frosted glass. Not Annabel. A male blur, gesturing to her impatiently.

"James!" She swung open the door, quite amazed. She had not thought they were on dropping-in terms. "What's wrong?"

"Wrong? Wrong? Nothingsh wrong—" He seemed to listen to himself, then took a deep breath and pulled back his shoulders. Unfortunately for his attempt at dignity, he had to exhale again.

Leonora tried not to flinch and reminded herself that her own breath couldn't be an improvement—not after Annabel's martinis. It seemed that heavy pre-luncheon drinking was a favorite hobby around Cosgreave Hall.

"Thank you." He strode past her. "I will come in for a few minutes. And perhaps a drink."

"I was just getting ready to go out." Leonora closed the door and followed him into the living-room uneasily. "I don't want to seem inhospitable, but Annabel and I were just going down to the hospital to visit Eddie."

"Poor Eddie." James sighed deeply. "My fault, all my fault. Poor chap had enough on his plate and I had to add to it. The final straw, shouldn't be shurprised."

"There's nothing final about it." Leonora tried to cheer him, he seemed to be sinking into the depths of a depression. "Eddie is doing well. They're just keeping him in for a few tests, that's all. He's allowed visitors. Why don't you come along with us to visit him?"

"No, no. Only add to his stress. Again. No. Give him my best—and my apologies. Abject apologies. Tell him I'll try to make it up to him. He'll understand. That's part of poor old Eddie's problem, actually. He's too unner—*under*standing."

"Eddie does seem to be a very nice man." Leonora hovered nervously as James stood in the center of the room and pivoted slowly, staring into every corner. "I'm glad he's recovering so well—and so quickly."

"Very fond of old Eddie," James agreed. He halted in mid-pirouette and quivered like a bird dog on point. "Let'sh drink to old Eddie." Unerringly, he made for the corner cupboard in which Leonora kept her small supply of liquor.

"Just a small one—" Leonora had the feeling that the situation was getting out of hand. James was behaving most strangely. She wondered how much he had already had to drink.

"Small one for you—" James brought out glasses and a bottle of Scotch—"an' a small one for me." He splashed a dollop into one glass and filled the other to the brim.

Leonora took the small one doubtfully, the Scotch would never mix with Annabel's martinis. Then she remembered that it didn't matter because she had no intention of drinking it. She was just . . . humouring James.

Since when had James needed humouring? He had always appeared to be one of the more sedate inhabitants, self-contained to the point of being uptight. Shy, pedantic, he had seemed to require coaxing along—not humouring. There was obviously another side to James—and she was discovering it now.

"James, I don't want to rush you, but I do have to leave. Why don't you come back later and we can tell you all about our visit with Eddie?"

"Right." James nodded owlishly. "Jusht one more drink, then we'll go visit Eddie."

"Why don't we have the drink when we get back?" Leonora hoped her smile did not look as false as it felt. "You know you're always welcome—"

"An' you're welcome, too. Only we haven't made you very welcome, have we? Been here all this time an' we haven't given you a proper houshwarming." He shook his head. "Mosht remish of ush." He poured himself another drink.

"You just make yourself at home." Leonora backed away slowly. "I have something that needs doing upstairs. I'll be back in a minute." She turned and fled up the stairs.

"Take your time," he called after her. She heard glass clink again.

"Annabel? Annabel, listen—" She had tried to dial silently, hoping that James would not pick up the sound.

"What? Who is this? Speak up, I can't hear you."

"It's me—Leonora. I'm whispering. I can't talk any louder."

"What's the matter?" Annabel was alert. "Something wrong?"

"Yes. No—I don't know. I'm not sure. James is here. Downstairs."

"James? Is he bothering you? Put him on."

"I can't. I'd rather not. He—he's behaving rather oddly. Can you hurry, Annabel? I—I think he's been drinking."

"Oh God! I'll be right there. Don't leave him alone. And, whatever you do, don't give him anything more to drink."

"Too late—" Leonora began, but Annabel had already slammed down the receiver and she was talking to the dialing tone.

Slowly, Leonora replaced her own receiver. So there *was* something about James and drink. Belatedly, she recalled her first meeting with James, when Eddie had come over to refill their glasses. She had been surprised when Eddie had accepted James's refusal of a top-up without even the customary polite insistence that a little more wouldn't hurt. It was obvious now that Eddie had known that it would hurt, that James had a drinking problem. Eddie had moved away so quickly that he had ignored her own empty glass—almost as though he were afraid of James and what he might do if he had one too many.

She discovered that she was just a little afraid of James herself. Annabel had told her not to leave him alone, but she was curiously reluctant to descend the stairs and go back to him. He was not the James Abercorn she had come to know—and she had the feeling that she did not wish to know this strange new James. She would rather wait until she heard Annabel at the door and they could go in to face James together.

But if James were to fall or do himself some sort of injury, it would be her fault. Annabel had had a note of peculiar urgency in her voice when she issued her instructions. She knew more about the circumstances than Leonora. They all did.

Also, she might be able to keep James from drinking still more. She had no illusions left—she knew that he was taking advantage of her absence to make inroads into her liquor supply. She saw now why he had come to call on her so abruptly: no one else would have allowed him access to their supply.

James had obviously finished his own and counted on the fact that she, as the newest member of the circle, had not yet been let into his little secret.

She paused at the top of the stairs to listen. He was moving around restlessly, but at least there were no more clinking noises. Had he had enough? Or had he emptied the bottle? Suddenly, there was complete and utter silence.

Leonora started down the stairs on tiptoe, suddenly reluctant to make any sound herself. If he had fallen asleep, she did not want to rouse him. She just wanted to get to the front door and look for Annabel. What was taking her so long?

Everything was awfully quiet in the living-room. She couldn't even hear him breathing.

With great relief, she saw Annabel's shadow looming on the other side of the frosted glass just as she reached the foot of the stairs. She hurried to open the door before Annabel could ring the doorbell.

"Where is he?" Annabel rushed in and looked around. "I warned you not to leave him alone."

"In the living-room. I think he's passed out. It's awfully quiet in there."

"Oh God! That's the most dangerous time! Never trust James when he goes too quiet." Annabel charged for the living-room, shaking her head.

"But—" Leonora was hot on her heels, frightened at what they might discover. "Why is James dangerous?"

"Shhh-" Annabel halted in the doorway and spoke softly. "You stand here and distract his attention. I'll slip round behind him."

"Why, James—" Leonora said weakly. "Whatever are you doing?"

"Houshwarming," James said. "Never gave you proper houshwarming to welcome you."

The flame of his cigarette lighter flickered just below the fringe of the curtains. He blinked over at Leonora in a way that suggested he was having difficulty focusing; that he was unsure of whether Annabel was actually there or whether he was seeing Leonora double.

"Oh, please don't bother," Leonora said. "I'm perfectly willing to take my welcome for granted."

"Good, good . . ." Annabel began to move away imperceptibly. "Keep him talking. Don't do anything to startle him . . ."

All very well for Annabel to say! How was she supposed to know what might startle or upset James? She was just beginning to realize how little she knew about him. About any of them, come to that.

Annabel was pussyfooting around the perimeter of the carpet like the last of the Mohicans.

James had begun twitching.

"Come and have another drink, James," Leonora said.

"Later." James shook his head. "After the Fire Brigade arrives." The flame trembled upwards toward the fringe. A thin strand sparked and shrivelled.

"That's right—" Leonora was rapidly becoming enlightened. "You didn't get to see the nice big red engines the other day, did you?"

"Don't be patronizing," James said coldly. "I'm not a fool."

Only a pyromaniac.

"We thought you were trying to put the fire out all by yourself—" Leonora continued along her trail of discovery. "But you weren't, were you? You were starting it. You didn't try to stop it until Eddie caught you. Eddie knew all along—" Probably all the residents had known it. She remembered now how they had all banded together to keep the houseparty guests away from James.

"Poor Eddie. Such a trial to him. You *will* give him my apologies, won't you. Wouldn't upshet poor old Eddie for the world."

"Of course I will. But why don't you come along and talk to him yourself?"

"Ah, no—" James waggled the cigarette lighter at her, the flame seemed to leap higher. "He won't want to shee me. Be reminded of hish troublesh. Needsh to concentrate on getting well." He gestured. The flame waved like a banner.

Annabel was circling closer. Leonora shifted to get into position to help her when she pounced. James was a tall, wiry man and Annabel was not young and was looking frailer by the minute. Leonora doubted the ability of both of them combined to wrestle James into submission.

She needn't have worried. Annabel had nothing so energetic in mind. Annabel took a final step forward, bent towards the cigarette lighter, took a deep breath—and blew. The flame went out.

"You—" James looked incredulously at the dead lighter. "You blew out my candle!"

"That's right," Annabel said. "We've blown out *all* the candles on the birthday cake. The party's over."

James slumped down on the sofa and buried his face in his hands. Annabel took the opportunity to pluck the lighter from his hand.

"No good . . ." James keened. "I'm no good. Unworthy . . . untrushtworthy . . . usheless . . ."

Leonora dashed over to make sure the curtains were not still smoldering. They seemed to be all right—apart from a few scorch marks.

"One . . . two . . . three . . ." Annabel was counting.

"No good . . . untrushtworthy . . . not worth powder to blow me to . . ."

"Four . . . five . . ."

James keeled over and passed out.

"Right on schedule," Annabel said. "He'll be all right now."

"You mean this happens all the time?" Now that the danger was over, Leonora found herself extremely annoyed. "You might have warned me."

"Sorry about that," Annabel said. "No—it doesn't happen all the time. Just now and again. He's been building up to it for some time, but I thought he'd got it out of his system at the weekend."

"*All* of you knew—" Some corner of her mind had been brooding about it all through this shambles. "You even expect it—" Her tone sharpened sarcastically. "Every now and again. And you don't even bother to warn strangers about him. The man is dangerous—he's a menace to the community. He—he ought to be put away!"

"You're upset." Annabel was maddeningly understanding. "Poor James is really only dangerous to himself. We try to keep a close watch over him. He'd be so miserable in an institution. In fact, that's his trouble. He was in one for far too long. That wretched boys' school where he taught. It did dreadful things to him. By the time he won the Pools and was able to take early retirement, it was just about too late. He tried to burn the school down to celebrate and it took a good chunk of his winnings to hush it up. Then he bought a tidy annuity and the flat over the old stables.

"And—" Annabel looked down at James thoughtfully—"I suspect he let Eddie invest the remainder for him. I also suspect Eddie didn't weather Meltdown Monday nearly so well as he tried to persuade us all that he did. No wonder James has been so fraught lately."

"*Fraught* is quite a good word for it."

"Oh well—" Annabel shrugged. "Time we were going." She started for the door.

"Oh no!" Leonora put her foot down. "I'm not going off and leaving *him* here. He might come to and decide to finish the job."

"Nonsense!" Annabel said. "He'll be perfectly all right

now. Except for being so pitifully hangdogish it will be painful to look at him for the next few days. You don't have to worry about James any more.''

"I'm not going to worry about him because I'm not going to go out and leave him here," Leonora said firmly. "In fact, even if I were staying around, I wouldn't want him here. Get rid of him."

"I think you're over-reacting," Annabel said patiently. "But I *do* take your point." She put a hand on James's shoulder and shook him slightly. "James! James! Wake up! Time to go home."

James snorted and settled deeper into the cushions. Annabel looked at Leonora with a helpless shrug.

"Get rid of him," Leonora repeated.

"Oh well . . ." Annabel shrugged again. "I suppose we could call Giles to come along and remove him."

"Fine," Leonora said. "He's had a lot of experience in shifting bodies recently."

"You know—" Annabel gave her a pained look—"you seem to have changed since you've been here. You're not so sweet and trusting as you were when you first arrived."

"I wonder why?" Leonora muttered.

"I think you'd better stay out of sight and let me handle Giles," Annabel decided. "He'll take James back to his own quarters and then we can go and tackle Eddie."

CHAPTER 17

"They've taken away my telephone," Eddie greeted them.

"Most people say 'hello' first," Annabel reproved.

"Hello-they've-taken-away-my-telephone. Make them give it back."

"Nonsense, Eddie!" Annabel dropped a kiss on his defenceless cheek. "If they've taken away your telephone, there's a reason. They probably want you to relax."

"How can I relax when I may be losing money?"

"Money isn't everything." No answer could have been more certain to madden him.

"That's all right for *you* to say!" Leonora only hoped that his temperature wasn't rising as fast as his voice.

"Hello, Eddie," she intervened quickly. "We came to see how you are."

He glared at them. *All the better for seeing you* was obviously not going to be the answer.

"We'd have stopped off and got you some grapes or something," Annabel said, "but we got thrown off schedule." She gave him a meaning look. "James has been at it again."

"Oh God, no!" Eddie groaned, falling back against the pillows. "What's the damage this time?"

143

"It's all right," Annabel said. "We caught him in time."

"It was *my* place he was trying to burn down." Leonora reminded them that she was the aggrieved party. "I must say, I think someone should have warned me about him. It was a nasty shock to walk in and find him setting fire to the curtains."

"I'm sorry," Eddie said. "We thought he'd be all right with you. He's usually all right with everybody—unless he's been drinking."

"He'd been drinking," Annabel said.

"I might have known it," Eddie groaned. "Why did I have to fall apart just now? All these irons in the fire and—"

"That's why," Annabel said crisply. "You've been taking too much on yourself again. You should delegate responsibility. Go in town to the office more often and take it easy."

"You sound like the doctor," Eddie grumbled.

"Wouldn't hurt to listen to him, Eddie. You land yourself with far too many problems."

"I can't help most of them," Eddie said. "They go with the territory."

"Precisely." Annabel looked down at him thoughtfully. "Eddie, has it ever occurred to you that it might be a good idea to start carving out a new territory?"

"How do you mean?"

But Annabel had turned to inspecting his bedside table. "We should have brought a Get-Well card," she said, picking up one of those already on display and checking the signature. "We'll have to send it to you."

"Don't bother," Eddie said. "I won't be hanging around here long enough to get it. As soon as I see the doctor this afternoon, I'm signing myself out."

"Do you think that's wise?" Annabel clearly didn't. "You're much better off resting comfortably here while they find out what went wrong with you."

"To hell with that!" Eddie said. "Nothing went wrong. I had a fainting fit, that's all. It could happen to anyone. They can't keep me here."

"Not if you don't want to stay," Annabel agreed amiably. "This isn't a prison."

Eddie gave a nervous start. He looked at Annabel warily.

"You don't look too well, Eddie." Annabel turned and pulled a chair over to the bedside. "Leonora, give him a glass of water."

Leonora poured out water from the jug on his bedside table. She suspected it would not be long before Eddie wished it were something stronger; she was beginning to recognize that gleam in Annabel's eye.

"Thanks." He took the glass, looked at it vaguely, and set it down again.

"Pull up a chair, Leonora," Annabel instructed. "No—on the other side of the bed, so that Eddie can see us both. Then we can have a nice visit."

Eddie grinned nervously. He was surrounded, beleaguered. He looked from one to the other, then to the doorway, as though for help. It was obvious that the last thing in the world he wanted was a nice visit with Annabel and Leonora.

"Bunty ought to be along any minute," he said hopefully. "Dinah, too. They said they'd come by after lunch."

"I shouldn't think so, Eddie." Annabel let him know that there was no escape that way. "They're playing bridge at Molly's this afternoon. They won't be along until quite a bit later."

"Bridge?" Eddie sat bolt upright. "But Bunty promised me—"

"Sorry, but I'm afraid the lure of the cardtable was greater than the call of the sickroom," Annabel said. "You can't blame her for that."

"Oh yes I can," Eddie said bitterly. "She promised me she'd give up those bridge parties. Her mother, too. Those women go out for blood when they play. I won't have any friends left."

"Oh, nonsense, Eddie. The friendly afternoon game has always been the lady's traditional way of supplementing her little allowance."

"Little!" Eddie was anguished. "Believe me, she doesn't need the money—"

And perhaps the others couldn't afford to lose it, Leonora thought suddenly. She was once again grateful for her teacher's long-ago warning. There was more than time to be lost at the bridge table.

"Little!" Eddie was fuming. "Do you know how much I give Bunty every month?"

"No—" Annabel's eyes gleamed. "How much?"

"Never mind." Eddie subsided against the pillows. "Look, it's awfully nice of you to bother to come to see me and I appreciate it. But I'm feeling kinda tired and—"

"Of course, you are, Eddie," Annabel smiled at him sweetly. "You've been wearing yourself out. It's hard work carrying bodies around."

Eddie closed his eyes and went very still. Leonora wondered if he was having another fainting fit. Or just a fit.

"That's right." Eddie opened his eyes, having decided on his story. "I usually seem to wind up carrying James home, don't I? I suppose I'll have him to thank for a slipped disc some day." His voice grew stronger as he saw Annabel nod understandingly. Perhaps he was convincing himself that that was what she had really meant.

"By the way—" he sat upright—"how did you manage James without me? Did he go home under his own steam?"

"Oh no," Annabel said. "He'd passed out, as usual. And you're right, he was too heavy for us to carry very far. So—" she smiled wickedly—"so we just dragged him out and left him under that bush near the gatepost. The one where the children made the little leafy cave. Such a popular place to leave a body, isn't it?"

Eddie relapsed. He fell back against the pillows, face

drained of all color. "Go away . . ." His voice was faint and seemed to come from a great distance. "I don't want to talk to you . . ."

"But *we* want to talk to *you*, Eddie." Annabel was relentless. "Now sit up and stop playing silly buggers! We didn't go near the bush with James. Whatever evidence was there is still there—undisturbed."

"There's no evidence!" Eddie sat up again.

"We called Giles to come and take James home." Annabel went on as though he hadn't spoken. "Giles is another expert at carting bodies around."

"You!" Eddie glared at Leonora. "You had to go and tell *her!*"

"Smartest thing she could have done," Annabel said. "If the rest of you had had sense enough to tell me in time, you wouldn't be in this mess now." She leaned forward in her chair and fixed him with a laserbeam stare. "Now tell me, where were you fool enough to try to hide the body?"

"I don't know what you're talking about," Eddie blustered weakly.

"Oh yes you do. And you're going to tell me if we have to sit here all night."

"You can't do that!" Eddie gasped, his resemblance to a cornered rat increasing.

"Oh yes we can." Annabel leaned back in her chair. "You know me, Eddie. So why don't you stop protecting Tessa and save yourself a lot of trouble?"

"Tessa?" Eddie might never have heard the name before. "Tessa? Tessa has nothing to do with it!" He glared at Leonora. "I've told you that before. Can't you get that idea out of your head?"

"If not Tessa, then who?" Annabel wanted to know.

"Nobody." Eddie tugged his sheet up around his chin as though planning to disappear beneath it. "You don't know what you're talking about.

"We're talking about Horton—the late Horton," Annabel said with a faint but well-judged air of menace.

Eddie was expecting it; his expression didn't change. "You're crazy," he said flatly. "You're both crazy."

"Are we? Suppose we were to report Horton as a missing person?"

"Go ahead. Horton's crazy, too. Nobody would be surprised at anything he did."

"Not even you, Eddie? You're not going to suggest that he hit himself over the head and crawled under that bush to die?"

"He isn't dead!" Eddie shouted. "Horton isn't dead! We told you that." He glared at Leonora again. "He was just knocked out. He came to when we were taking him home."

"Then where is he now?" Annabel shook her head. "You'll have to come up with a better story than that, Eddie. It won't hold water. No one has seen Horton since Friday night."

"I don't know where he is, but he isn't dead."

"Perhaps he isn't," Leonora said. "But somebody was. I suppose—" She took a deep breath and shot her bolt. "I suppose it was Tom."

"Tom?" Eddie's eyes widened. "Tom who?"

"There's another man missing," Leonora pointed out. "Clio's husband. Tom Warriner. Everyone agrees that he's been gone longer than usual on his business trip. He's way overdue back. Perhaps he *did* come back and . . . met with some kind of accident. Maybe he was the one who was lying dead under that bush."

"Good thinking," Annabel approved. "I was just about to bring up that possibility myself."

"My God!" Eddie was aghast. "No wonder you're both widows! You must have driven a couple of poor guys to their early graves. And they must have been damned relieved to get there!"

"Edward!" Annabel's face was thunderous. "That was unforgivable! Apologize immediately!"

"Okay, okay, I'm sorry. I'm overwrought. I'm—" Eddie was groping for something under his pillow, a sudden crafty look on his face. Annabel stood up and bent over him, but she was too late. He was stabbing frantically at the bellpush in his hand. "I'm getting you out of here!"

Either Eddie tipped awfully well or the nurse was under his spell. She appeared in the doorway before Annabel could wrench the bellpush away from him. It was a good try, but the struggle had left Annabel sprawled across the bed in a faintly compromising position.

"Is everything all right here?" the nurse asked quickly.

"Yes," Annabel said.

"No!" Eddie said. "I—I feel terrible." He looked terrible, pale and gasping. "I—I'm having a relapse. I think I'm dying. Help me!"

The nurse rushed to him, brushing Annabel aside. She took his pulse, dividing severe glances between Annabel and the fob watch pinned to her bib.

Annabel, who could read the handwriting on the wall as well as the next one, was already gathering up her handbag.

"I'm afraid you'll have to leave now." The nurse confirmed Annabel's diagnosis. "The patient needs absolute rest and quiet." Her frown implied that he would get neither so long as Annabel was around.

"Just leaving," Annabel said. "Goodbye, Eddie, dear. We'll come to see you at home. This afternoon, didn't you say?"

"He won't be home this afternoon," the nurse snapped.

"No, no," Eddie said. "I'm having a relapse. I'm staying here. They're going to stop me having *any* visitors. Tell Bunty to ring in the morning and see if they'll let even her come then."

"We've got him on the run," Annabel said gleefully as they descended the front steps of the hospital.

"I'd say it was the other way around."

"I've been thrown out of better places than this."

Leonora believed it. "Anyway, so much for Eddie being the weakest link. He might be, but we're not going to get near him again for a long time. What do you want to bet that he stays in that private room until he has to leave for the cruise liner?"

"Only too likely, I'm afraid. Especially if he can talk them into giving him back his telephone."

"So what do we do now? Tackle Clio?"

"God, no! I mean, we wouldn't want to upset her. She worries enough about Tom as it is. She's so . . . delicately balanced."

"Not another one!"

"Her health, I mean, is fragile." Annabel's airy laugh was unconvincing. "We wouldn't want two of them in hospital."

"What's wrong with her?" Leonora was prepared to believe that Clio might have a health problem. There was something too uncertain, too fey about her. "Nerves?"

"Nothing like that," Annabel said absently. "Don't let me forget to give Eddie's message to Bunty. Poor Eddie. Always so concerned about her. She doesn't deserve it."

"Why not?"

"Eddie is sweet—and perhaps a bit naïve when it comes to anything except financial wizardry. Let's just say I do hope he isn't making plans for his Silver Wedding celebrations."

"They haven't been married that long, have they?" Leonora was momentarily puzzled. Eddie must be in his early forties and Bunty could not be much more than thirty-five.

"No, no, I just meant it as a general observation. He's her second husband, you know."

"Yes, you told me. The children are his, aren't they?"

"Oh yes. Such a relief to Bunty now that they're old enough to be sent away to school. Only just, mind you. I wouldn't have sent mine away that young, but Bunty—" She quirked an eyebrow and rolled her eyes.

"It sounds as though Bunty isn't bothered by the empty nest syndrome."

"Bothered by it? She positively encourages it. Once a bolter, always a bolter. She and Eddie have been married for ten years now. For Bunty, that's a record."

"And that's why you don't think Eddie should make any plans for their Silver Wedding."

"I may be wrong—" Annabel didn't believe it for a minute. "But I think I've detected signs of restlessness lately. Eddie may be tempting Fate if he arranges a nice romantic cruise."

"You think Bunty may elope with one of the other passengers?"

"One of the officers, more likely. They'll be looking very handsome in their tropical uniforms."

"Not to mention those tropical nights under a big Mediterranean moon—" Leonora caught herself sounding wistful and stopped abruptly.

"Well, that's Eddie's problem." Annabel dismissed the vision. "Our problem is still that missing corpse." They were at the car now. Annabel unlocked the door and slid in behind the steering-wheel.

"Where are we going now?" Leonora got in beside her.

"I was just wondering—" Annabel started the engine—"if we could manage to get a look at the wine cellar under Cosgreave Hall."

CHAPTER 18

Annabel left the car in front of her own cottage and they walked up to Cosgreave Hall, circling it first.

"You're not going to try to break in here, are you?" Leonora asked uneasily. She had the feeling that Annabel would dare anything.

"Not in broad daylight," Annabel said indignantly, quite as though that had stopped her earlier. "Be dark soon, though. Pity everyone is home now. Perhaps after midnight . . ."

"You can't," Leonora protested. "Suppose someone caught you. *This* house is occupied—very occupied."

"Suppose you're right," Annabel admitted reluctantly. "It *would* be awkward to run into Dinah and have to explain . . ." She trailed off, unwilling to admit even to herself the explanations that would have to be made. "No, we'll have to do it another way."

Their circuit of the house completed, Annabel led the way up to the front door and rang the bell. Lady Cosgreave opened the door herself.

"Annabel, come in. And Leonora. I saw you prowling around out there and wondered what you were doing."

"We've been to see Eddie," Annabel said. "Got a message from him for you: no more visitors today. He's had a relapse."

"Was that before or after you got there?" Lady Cosgreave had no illusions about her old friend. "No, come and have a drink and tell me what you were looking for out there. I haven't seen anyone studying the house from the outside so thoroughly since the time we had that American antiquarian scholar counting all the windows trying to discover a hidden room. Some legend or other he thought he could trace to Cosgreave Hall. All nonsense, of course; if there were a hidden room, we'd have known about it."

It was an enormous house. Leonora felt a chill of despair. Was Lady Cosgreave insinuating that the body was hidden in it somewhere, in a secret room? Was she challenging them to find it?

"Nonsense, indeed." Annabel was unperturbed. "This house isn't old enough to have any legends. Although—" she aimed a careful shot across her friend's bow—"it might acquire one soon. It's early days yet, as houses go. You might even pick up a ghost or two—the way things are going."

"Have a glass of sherry, Annabel." Lady Cosgreave ignored provocation—or did she? "We have manzanilla, fino, barbarillo, amontillado, oloroso . . ."

"No gin?" Annabel surveyed the ranged bottles with disfavor.

"Do try and be civilized, Annabel," Lady Cosgreave sighed. "*We* drink sherry before dinner. There are six different varieties on offer. There must be *one* you could force yourself to drink instead of gin."

"'Force' would be the word." Annabel sulked for a moment, then her face brightened. "I'd prefer almost anything to sherry. I'll bet you keep some interesting wines in your cellar. You wouldn't dare let guests browse around down there and choose for themselves."

"Why, Annabel," Lady Cosgreave said sweetly, "why didn't you simply *say* you'd like to inspect the cellar. You're perfectly welcome to—we have nothing to hide. Let me show you the way. You too, Leonora. Just come along."

Lady Cosgreave led the way with such alacrity that they knew there was nothing but wine to be found in the wine cellar. If anything else had ever been there, it had been cleared safely out of the way.

"Hah! Knew I could find something better than that sherry!" Out of sheer spite, Annabel pounced on a vintage champagne, the bottle so shrouded in dust and cobwebs that it was certain to be one of the rarest and most expensive items in the cellar.

"*Dear* Annabel—" Lady Cosgreave paled. "Your taste hasn't entirely abandoned you, but perhaps we can find you your bottle of gin, after all. I'm afraid I was teasing you just a little."

"This will be fine." Annabel clung grimly to the bottle, blowing at it and raising a cloud of dust.

It was a battle of Titans. Leonora concentrated on keeping her profile so low it was practically subliminal. This good intention was rather marred by the coughing fit induced by all that dust.

"No, no—" Lady Cosgreave coughed, reaching out and getting a firm grip on the bottle. "I couldn't be so inhospitable as to make you drink this stuff when you really crave gin. Come upstairs and we'll find the gin for you."

"No, no—I've decided you're right." Annabel kept hold of the bottle. "It's time I broadened my horizons. There is more to life than gin. Champagne will do for a start." She blew off another layer of dust. "A few more puffs and I'll even be able to read the label."

A brief wrestling match ensued, but Annabel remained in possession of the bottle.

"All right, Annabel," Lady Cosgreave said. "You've made your point. Now put it back in the rack. It's too shaken up for us to be able to open it for days yet."

"Weeks, more likely." Annabel squinted complacently at the bottle, which looked as though it were seething inwardly, and replaced it in the rack. "Too bad. It looks as though I might have enjoyed it. Quite some age, isn't it?"

"One of the last of the vintages laid down by my dear husband." Lady Cosgreave lost no time herding them back upstairs. "Dear Eddie has done much toward replenishing the wine cellar, but most of his stocks are still too young to drink. And, of course, he had to stop for a while because of The Crash.

"Never mind—" she led them into the drawing-room. "The Market is doing well again, our little hiccough is over, and there'll be some interesting wine auctions at Sotheby's and Christie's again in the future."

"Meanwhile, where's the gin?" Annabel was sticking to the point.

Where's the body? was a more pertinent point, Leonora felt. But Lady Cosgreave would never answer such a question; she might not even know the answer. She had not been here at the time of the death, she had arrived later. Neither Bunty nor Eddie had ever struck Leonora as particularly confiding characters. They had probably told Lady Cosgreave as much as they felt it necessary for her to know—and no more.

It was also possible that Lady Cosgreave did not wish to know everything. What she didn't know, she couldn't tell—or let slip inadvertently. And, as an old friend of the Chief Constable, she obviously had more opportunities for dangerous indiscretion than she would have with less highly placed nonofficial friends.

At least the body was not in the wine cellar and Lady Cosgreave had known it, which must mean that she had been assured that it had not been hidden anywhere in the house. An extremely wise precaution. Leonora was relieved to know that Annabel would not have to exercise her house-breaking talents on Cosgreave Hall. Her relief ended abruptly as she turned and saw Lady Cosgreave watching her speculatively.

"Tell me, my dear—" Lady Cosgreave gave her a sherry— "I've been meaning to ask before. How is your painting coming along?"

"Very well, thank you," Leonora said warily.

"You must give us a private showing before you send your pictures on for Exhibition," Lady Cosgreave decreed.

"Yes, I must," Leonora murmured, intending no such thing.

"Do you know, I don't even know what sort of painting you do. I trust it's not abstract?"

"No." Too late, Leonora became aware that she should not have given Lady Cosgreave even that much encouragement. "I don't do abstracts."

"I thought not!" Lady Cosgreave was triumphant. "You're much too sensible. Landscapes, I was sure. And portraits—do you paint portraits?"

"No." Leonora continued fighting a losing battle. "I don't paint portraits."

"Oh, but my dear, you should. There's *such* a market for them. I'm sure I could put some quite good commissions your way. Of course—" she preened—"you'd need an example of your work to show them. If you haven't done any portraits before—"

"I'm not a portrait painter."

"There's also a splendid market in pictures of the ancestral home and grounds," Lady Cosgreave persisted. "Hereward was saying just the other day that there have been so many changes in his estate since the Gainsborough that he really ought to get another painting done before the end of the century to record the changes for posterity."

"Gainsborough?" Leonora gasped faintly.

"One of his usual catchpenny efforts," Lady Cosgreave said airily. "You know the sort of thing, my dear. The family and pets assembled in front of the family home with the ancestral acres rolling away into infinity behind them. At least it's an improvement on all those frightful Lely portraits of the female ancestors, all bulging eyes and Mick Jagger mouths. Thank heavens Hereward and dear Tessa didn't inherit any of those characteristics—except that it was all Lely, wasn't it? The entire female aristocracy of England at that time surely couldn't have consisted of human versions of King Charles spaniels.''

"Stand firm," Annabel muttered under her breath. "Don't weaken." But Leonora was hooked and they both knew it.

"You really must see Hereward's collection," Lady Cosgreave smirked, scenting victory. "His Long Gallery isn't open to the public, but I can arrange a visit for you. He'd be delighted to give you tea and show you around. Shall I arrange it for next week?"

"Oh yes, please. That would be marvelous." Leonora was still gasping. A private collection of ancestrally-commissioned paintings, *in situ* for generations. Gainsborough, Lely—and how many others? It was an opportunity beyond her wildest dreams. She almost felt that no price would be too great to pay.

"And you really must give serious consideration to trying portraiture yourself," Lady Cosgreave directed. "I'd be happy to sit for you while you practise a bit."

"Trust Dinah to work it so that she gets something for nothing," Annabel grumbled as soon as they were out of earshot. "You shouldn't let her get away with it."

"I know, I know," Leonora moaned. "I don't know whether I've been bribed or blackmailed—but it was just too much to resist."

"I might have known it," Annabel sighed. "Dinah has a genius for finding someone's weakness and using it against them."

"Wait a minute—" Leonora was listening to the echo of what she herself had just said. "Blackmail!" The word suddenly shed a whole new light on the situation. "Blackmail!"

"Blackmail?" Annabel was startled. "What do you mean?"

"Don't you see? That would explain why Eddie was so horrified when I thought Tessa had hit Horton with her car. He knew she was innocent—because Horton hadn't died by accident. He'd been killed—by one of his victims. One of the people he'd been blackmailing."

"Well," Annabel said grudgingly, "I suppose I *could* see Horton as a blackmailer. He was certainly the type."

Leonora had the impression that Annabel was vexed because she had not thought of the idea herself.

"There are certainly enough reasons for blackmail around here." Leonora began ticking them off on her fingers. "The Carmodys aren't married—and they're of an age group to whom that sort of thing was important. Look at the way they're trying to keep up appearances by giving the impression that they are.

"James is a pyromaniac—with plenty of money from his Pools win. He tried to burn down his own school as a farewell gesture. The newspapers would love that story, even if it is a bit old. And he's still setting fire to places as soon as he has one drink too many.

"Then Eddie seems to be in financial deep water, although he keeps giving extravagant parties for all his friends, obviously trying to give the impression that he has no financial worries at all. But let the newspapers get a whiff of possible trouble and they'd be down on him like a bunch of—of *paparazzi*. And any hints in the financial columns might provoke the Securities Exchange Commission—or the Fraud Squad—to begin an investigation into his affairs."

"You might be right." Annabel began to get into the spirit of the thing. "And then there's—" She broke off and started again, leaving Leonora with the further impression that she had started to say something else—and that there was probably still more that she had to find out about her neighbors in the manorial enclave.

"There's the way Horton kept hanging around his old cottage," Annabel said triumphantly. "Perhaps he wasn't just trying to make the new tenants uncomfortable enough to leave—although that probably came into it, too. He was spying on them, to find out if they had any secrets he could blackmail them about."

"That's possible," Leonora agreed, still wondering what Annabel had decided to conceal. Had it to do with her old friend Dinah? Or was there something in Annabel's own past? Was Annabel another of Horton's victims?

It was very difficult to picture Annabel as a Victim. Leonora suspected she was more of the "Publish-and-be-damned" persuasion. But there were others . . .

"What about Lady Cosgreave's past?" she asked. "You seem to think she's setting her cap at Hereward. Is there anything in her background that she'd pay to keep him from finding out?"

"Dinah?" Annabel snorted. "Dinah's life is an open gossip column. All anyone who's missed any episodes has to do is go out to the Colindale Newspaper Library and read the microfilm files. She was one of the best-documented women of her generation. Believe me, there'd be no point in Horton's attempting to blackmail Dinah—she'd have laughed in his face."

"If it *was* Horton." Leonora returned to her earlier theory.

"Yes, there *is* that," Annabel said thoughtfully. "I wonder if Tom Warriner has returned from his business trip yet?"

"But why should anyone kill *him?* And why should Molly and all the others lie about it and hide the body?"

"I don't know why anyone would want to kill him—I'll have to think about that. But I can understand why they'd want to hide the body. To keep Clio from seeing it and getting upset."

"What good would that do? She'd have to find out her husband was dead—sooner or later."

"Perhaps they wanted to decide how to break the news to her gently." Annabel looked thoughtful. "They were playing for time . . ."

"And perhaps they weren't going to tell her at all," Leonora suggested sharply.

"Eddie has such a kind heart—" Annabel began.

"Kind? Do you think it's kind to leave Clio worrying and wondering why her husband hasn't come back? I *do* think a woman has a right to know whether she's a widow or not."

"Yes, yes, of course, she does." Annabel spoke in such a hushed soothing tone that it reminded Leonora that she was still masquerading as a widow herself. She spared a moment to curse Lady Cosgreave silently.

"Why don't we pop up and call on Clio?" Annabel brightened. "Perhaps Tom has come home by now. Then we'd know that Molly wasn't lying when she identified the body as Horton."

"Oh, it's you." Clio's face fell as she opened the door. "I'm sorry," she added quickly. "I didn't mean that the way it sounded. Of course I'm glad to see you. Come in."

"We don't want to intrude—" Annabel was already inside the hall—"if you're expecting someone?"

"Only the telephone repairman," Clio sighed. "But I suppose it's much too late for him to come now. I've been waiting in all day for him. They promised faithfully—"

"They always do," Annabel sympathized. "What's wrong with your telephone?"

"Oh, the usual thing." Clio sighed again. "At first, I could make calls out all right, so I didn't realize that no calls were coming in. I didn't know anything was wrong until Molly told me that she'd been trying to get me but thought I must be out because the phone kept ringing and I didn't answer. I was here all the time, of course."

"How annoying." Annabel was looking around the hall.

There was no sign of a returning traveller; no suitcase, brief-case or umbrella.

"As soon as she told me, I rang up and complained and they promised to send round an engineer. They haven't—and now the line is completely dead. I can't even make calls out any more. It's maddening."

"It certainly is," Annabel agreed, following Clio into the sitting-room. "Would you like to come down and use my telephone?"

"Thanks, but I'd better stay here. Tom might be back at any moment. I suppose he's been trying to get through to tell me why he's been delayed. He'll be worrying terribly by now, wondering where I am. If he comes back and I'm not here, he'll be frantic."

Annabel and Leonora carefully refrained from exchanging glances. It was possible. It was almost most unfortunate that the telephone had gone out of order at this particular time. Briefly, Leonora wondered if one of the conspirators could have cut the outside wire. That would account for the phone being totally dead now—and it would also keep Clio from worrying unduly, thus buying them more time. But why did they need all this extra time?

"But you're not worried about Tom?" Annabel prodded. "Wasn't he due back over a week ago?"

"Yes, but—" Clio gave a brave, tremulous smile—"it wouldn't be the first time he's changed his mind and forgotten to let me know. He gets so involved in his business . . . and he knows I'll be sensible about it."

Not for the first time, Leonora felt a wave of sympathy for Clio. Tom Warriner sounded like a selfish, thoughtless brute who probably deserved to be murdered. If he treated other people the way he treated his wife, it would not be surprising if he wound up lying under the bushes with his head bashed in.

"He ought to have let you know." Annabel frowned. "At the very least, he might have sent a telegram."

"Perhaps he did," Clio said. "Remember, they don't send them round immediately any more. They just pop them into the post for delivery the next day—and you know what the post can be like."

"Oh yes." Annabel shuddered. "Wildcat strikes, go-slows, sulks and tears. If someone doesn't like the way their tea is brewed, it can mean a walkout and a postal backlog—and God knows when any of us will see our post again."

"Exactly," Clio sighed. "It's all so unsatisfactory. And there's nothing we can do about it."

"I know what I'd like to do," Annabel said grimly. "Unfortunately, there's a law against it."

"Such a bore." Clio sighed again. "But let's talk of something more pleasant. I saw the two of you setting off on your sketching expedition this morning? Did you have a successful day?"

"Not very," Annabel said. "We're still looking for the perfect spot."

"There must be plenty of them around. If I were sketching, I'd go down by the weir. Of course, trying to capture all that rushing water would be much too advanced for me—and probably for you, too. But Leonora ought to be able to do it."

"That's a thought," Annabel said. "We'll try there tomorrow."

"I wish I could come with you." Clio was wistful.

"Why don't you?" Leonora momentarily forgot that it wouldn't be an ordinary sketching party. Annabel's frown reminded her.

"I can't. I have to wait here for the telephone engineer. And even if he comes first thing in the morning and repairs the phone, I'll still have to stay around in case Tom is trying to reach me. Anyway—" she brightened—"the forecast is for rain tomorrow. Heavy rain. So you won't be going out, either."

*   *   *

"That husband of hers sounds ghastly," Leonora said, as soon as they were away from the East Wing. "I don't know how she puts up with that treatment."

"Don't worry," Annabel said drily. "Clio has little ways of making her displeasure felt when he's been playing her up too badly."

"Oh, really?" Leonora discovered a sudden depth of cynicism in herself that had not existed before she took up residence at Cosgreave Hall. "What does *she* set fire to? The bed?"

"No, no," Annabel assured her. "Clio would never do anything so violent."

"You mean she just invites James in, gives him a few drinks and lets him do the dirty work?"

"You know," Annabel said thoughtfully, "you're acquiring a nasty suspicious mind."

"It must be something in the air," Leonora said.

"You need an early night," Annabel decided. "Go straight to bed, get plenty of sleep and I'll call round for you in the morning and we'll try the weir."

"It's going to rain tomorrow." For once, Leonora was delighted at the prospect. It had been an awfully long day and she was exhausted; keeping pace with Annabel wasn't easy.

"Oh well—" Annabel frowned—"I suppose one more day won't matter at this point. Day after tomorrow, then?"

"All right." Leonora had the impression that Annabel was not entirely displeased. Perhaps she had reached the limits of her own stamina; even her diamonds were looking subdued. A day to recover would do them both good.

"Yes, Friday—weather permitting."

CHAPTER 19

"Off again?" Bunty greeted them with an indulgent smile as they all met on Friday morning. "Can I give you a lift anywhere?" She was driving and had slowed by the gateposts to check the traffic before turning into the road.

"No, thank you," Annabel said. "We don't know where we're going. We just want to find a pretty spot where Leonora can set up her easel and I can sketch."

"How nice," Bunty said. "It *is* good to see you taking an interest in a hobby, Annabel. I'm sure it will do you a world of good."

"You're off early, aren't you?" Annabel gave her an oversweet smile.

"I'm going for Eddie. He's fed up with all those dreary tests and things and wants to come home. And we have guests arriving for the weekend. He'll have to be here."

"Do you think that's wise?" Annabel asked. "Mightn't the excitement be too much for him? The quacks haven't really got to the bottom of what was ailing him, have they? Shouldn't he be resting and taking it easy?"

"You know Eddie," Bunty said blithely. "He can't bear inactivity. It would do him far more harm to be left out of

165

things. He'd brood and fret and work himself into a state. Far better to have him back here. Mummy and I will keep an eye on him and make sure he doesn't overdo.''

''You don't have intensive care equipment,'' Annabel pointed out. ''He shouldn't stray too far from that until they've pinpointed what went wrong the other night.''

''Perhaps not, but the doctors have agreed he can leave. So they can't be too concerned.'' Bunty gave a cheery wave, gunned the motor and shot out into the main road.

''She may be right,'' Leonora said. ''If the doctors aren't worried, why should you be?''

''Don't like it,'' Annabel said. ''Eddie's at a dangerous age, too sedentary, been under a lot of stress. What happened could have been a warning. He was lucky that it happened when there were people around him. If it had happened in the middle of the night, up there in that turret room, alone, with those damned computers telling him the Market was nosediving again and there was another International Crisis . . .''

''Yes, he would be better off to stay where he is for a few more days. In fact,'' Leonora smiled, ''I thought you'd fixed that. I got the distinct impression that Eddie wasn't anxious to get within questioning range of either of us for a long time. He won't be able to hide behind Bunty as successfully as he was able to hide behind the medical staff.''

''Don't be too sure of that,'' Annabel said. ''Bunty can be quite devious in her own quiet way. And Dinah will back her. Together, they make quite a formidable pair. Eddie could find worse skirts to hide behind.''

''But he'll still have to show himself in public and make some sort of effort if they're having another party this weekend.''

''True, but Bunty and Dinah will keep the stress level as low as possible. They know which side their bread is buttered on. For one thing—'' Annabel's tone was sardonic—''we can count on a quiet weekend to ourselves. They won't be inviting *us* up to join the party.''

"Good," Leonora said heartily. "I want to get some work done."

"If that's a hint," Annabel said, "I suppose we can call off the search for the weekend. It wouldn't be much good, anyway, with the guests charging all over the place. So we'd better try to cover as much territory as possible today. We'll go downstream along the towpath and inspect the weir. I should have thought of it myself, but I wanted to check the house first. This way—" She started for the towpath.

"Could we go into town first?" Leonora remembered and pulled a sheet of paper from her pocket. "Clio popped this through my letter-box this morning. Very early. I found it when I came downstairs. Her phone is still out. She wants us to order some supplies for her. We could get that out of the way first and have the rest of the day to search."

"What supplies?" Annabel took the list curiously and read it. "Mmm, the greengrocer's, the butcher's, the chemist . . . all right, that shouldn't take long."

The first two didn't. It wasn't until the girl in the chemist's shop was parcelling up their order that they ran into difficulty.

"And if you'd just deliver it to—" Leonora began.

"I'm sorry, madam, we don't deliver."

"But—" Leonora looked at the parcel in dismay. Clio had ordered a box of paper handkerchiefs, a large bottle of aspirins, hair spray, shampoo and two kinds of toothpaste. The parcel was not going to be very heavy, but it was bulky. "But we can't carry that around with us all day."

"I'm sorry, madam. We don't deliver," the girl repeated.

"But—" Leonora tried again to protest.

"We don't—"

"Quite all right," Annabel said briskly. "We won't bother, then. The things are only for Mrs. Warriner. She'll just have to come down herself and pick up what she wants."

"Oh no!" The girl blanched. "I didn't know they were for Mrs. Warriner. That's different. In that case, we will deliver."

"I felt sure you would," Annabel said sweetly. "Come, Leonora." She turned on her heel and they left the shop before the girl could change her mind.

"I don't see why Clio rates all this special attention," Leonora said, a trifle enviously. "Why won't they deliver for everyone?"

"Never mind," Annabel said. "We've wasted enough time in town. We can cut through this alley to the towpath . . ."

It was a longer, muddier walk to the weir than Leonora had expected. She wished that she had worn a sturdier pair of shoes. Annabel plowed ahead steadily, but seemed rather abstracted and not inclined towards conversation. That suited Leonora; the towpath was rougher and less-travelled this way, she had to concentrate on watching her step.

They could hear the weir long before they could see it. The flow of the river accelerated as the water rushed towards the weir. Annabel picked up speed, too.

"Come on," she called. "It's not far now."

"You go ahead." The game wasn't worth a broken ankle. "I'm right behind you."

Annabel waved an acknowledgement over her shoulder and plunged ahead. The sun had disappeared and the sky was darkening rapidly; it looked as though it might rain again. The roar of rushing water grew louder. Suddenly, Annabel was no longer in sight.

"Annabel?" Leonora called anxiously.

A hand appeared above some tufts of grass and waved. Leonora went forward cautiously.

"Annabel, be careful!" The river bank was steeper and more slippery here than it had been farther upstream. The water was deeper and the current faster. Heedless of all this, Annabel was scrambling down the bank to the river's edge.

"Come down," Annabel looked up and urged. "You can't see properly from up there."

"What is it? Have you found something?" Fighting for balance, Leonora slid down the bank.

"Thought I spotted something—" Annabel had found another stick and was prodding the rushes.

"Don't!" Leonora gasped in sudden revulsion. She didn't want to see what Annabel might bring to the surface. Not after several days' immersion in water.

"Steady on," Annabel said. "It's probably just another false alarm." She continued prodding with renewed vigor. She didn't believe it was a false alarm at all.

Leonora took a step back as something broke free of the mud, surfaced, turned over and sank again.

"Don't run away. It isn't what you're thinking. It's much too small."

"I'm not running away." Leonora forced herself to stand firm. There was something ghoulish about Annabel's glee as she repeated her dredging operation. This time the object bobbed on the surface long enough to be identified as a man's shoe before it began drifting out into midstream.

"Don't fall in!" Annabel had leaned out trying to hook it out of the water with her stick.

"I won't—" Annabel stretched out her free hand—"if you'll just hang on to me. I've almost got it."

Leonora clutched desperately at Annabel's hand and dug in her heels to take most of Annabel's weight.

"Almost got it—" Annabel cheered herself on. "Almost . . . almost . . . Got it!" With a triumphant flourish, she lifted the stick with the shoe on the end of it. It hovered over the water for a moment, then flipped ashore like a landed trout, falling at Leonora's feet.

"Oh!" It had landed sole upwards. Leonora had seen that strange triangular mark on the sole before.

"Recognize it?" Annabel regained her balance with a tug that nearly lost Leonora hers.

"Yes. He . . . he was wearing it . . . under the bush."

"Thought so!" Annabel produced a plastic carrier bag and, still using the stick, slid the shoe into it. "He *was* dumped into the river then. Most sensible place, after all. Let's go down below the weir and see if we can find the body." She loped off along the towpath again with far more enthusiasm than Leonora felt.

The first splashes of rain began pockmarking the surface of the river. Annabel took no notice. Not even when the rain intensified and gave every indication of being a repeat of yesterday's steady downpour did she appear to notice.

"Annabel, let's go back. It's raining."

"Little rain never hurt anybody." Absently Annabel lifted the plastic bag to shield her hairdo while Leonora shivered with revulsion.

"Annabel!"

"What's the matter? Oh—" Annabel suddenly realized what she had done and lowered the bag reluctantly. "You Americans are too sensitive," she grumbled.

"We are also not waterproof." Leonora was glad of the excuse to call off the expedition. "I don't know what you're going to do, but I'm going back."

"Oh, all right." They were already below the weir and there was nothing to be seen. The small whirlpool at the foot of the waterfall was buffeting nothing but a few branches.

"We could use a drink—" Annabel brightened—"to ward off a chill. If there was ever anything here, it must be a lot farther downstream by now."

"And we can call the police—?" Leonora ventured.

"Police? Whatever for? We haven't any proof. All we have is a piece of the jigsaw. They'd laugh us out of the station if we waggled a shoe at them and tried to convince them it meant a crime had been committed. Do you know how many shoes you might drag out of the river at any given time? Although," Annabel added judiciously, "not many of them would be handmade shoes, I grant you."

"Handmade shoes? Horton?"

''There *is* that.'' Annabel was still in judicious mood. ''Tom Warriner—and most of the other men around here— would have handmade shoes. But that doesn't really get us any forwarder, you see, because they often gave their cast-offs to Horton. He took an average size in everything, so he did rather well. There were times when he was better dressed than some of his benefactors.''

''So we still don't know which one was the victim.''

''No, but we're that much ahead.'' Annabel struck out along the towpath, perhaps impelled by visions of the jug of martinis at the end of the track. ''We'll go over the shoe with a fine-tooth comb when we get back and see if we can learn anything more from it.''

''I'd rather not,'' Leonora said faintly.

Annabel did not deign to hear her.

The first cars were turning into the driveway as they arrived back at Cosgrave Hall. One or two drivers waved at them, but no one stopped to offer them a lift up the drive. They were drenched by this time and would have imperilled the upholstery; it was really rather sporting of the drivers to acknowledge their presence at all.

''My place,'' Annabel directed, presumably not trusting Leonora's supply of gin.

Behind them, an oncoming car slowed abruptly and so noticeably that they both turned to look at it. Tessa Andrews drove past the gateposts at a crawl and raised a timid hand to them once she was safely into the drive.

''She's sober enough this time,'' Annabel said. ''Learned her lesson, I dare say.''

''It's a different car,'' Leonora observed.

''Other one's probably still in the garage getting those dents hammered out.''

The evidence destroyed . . . Leonora waved back, feeling hypocritical.

"You go and change out of those wet clothes," Annabel said. "Then come over to me."

But, once inside, Leonora suddenly felt too exhausted to face any more socializing that day, far less any of Annabel's martinis. The house was warm and pleasant; she had a leisurely bath, then wrapped herself firmly in her bathrobe and went downstairs to the kitchen. She lit the gas and made a cup of tea and carried it into the living-room. After she finished it, she would ring Annabel with her excuses.

The rain had settled in for the rest of the day, perhaps the weekend, strumming against the windows soporifically. Outside, another high-powered car roared up the drive. Bunty would have her work cut out to keep her guests amused throughout a wet weekend.

Idly, Leonora got up and wandered over to look out of the window. She was just in time to see Bunty's car round the curve, with Bunty driving very carefully so as not to jolt her precious passenger.

Eddie was home.

She rang Annabel, who took the news that she was cancelling their arrangement with equanimity.

"It might be just as well," Annabel said. "I've been thinking—and what I think is that this would be a good time to call on Molly and Giles and have a quiet chat."

"But I don't want to go out at all," Leonora protested. "Not just to your place—anywhere. I want to stay at home and get on with my work."

"And so you shall. I didn't mean you to come. I'll get far more out of them if I'm by myself. We've known each other for a long time. They'll talk more freely to me."

"Are you . . ." Leonora felt a distinct qualm. Should she let Annabel go alone? But Annabel was right: they would speak more freely to her. "Are you going to confront them with . . . the evidence?"

"The shoe?" Annabel laughed. "Certainly not. I'll leave

that here. Well hidden. That's the ace up our sleeve.''

"Annabel—this isn't a game." Molly and Giles guarded their respectability jealously, as did the others at Cosgreave Hall. They were all people who had much to lose.

"Annabel—be careful."

"I'm always careful," Annabel said, not strictly accurately.

CHAPTER 20

The sudden sharp peal of the doorbell made Leonora jump. Worse, it made her hand jerk and a delicate line skidded almost off the page and in the wrong direction. She glared down at it in annoyance. The sketch wasn't ruined, but it was definitely marred. Thank goodness she hadn't been working in ink. Abstractedly, she reached for the eraser.

The doorbell pealed again, bringing her back to the instant. That would be Annabel, of course, come to report on her talk with Molly and Giles. She tossed the sketchpad on the table and hurried to the door.

"All right—" She swung open the door. "What did you—? Oh!"

"Good afternoon," Lady Cosgreave stood there, looking formidable. "May I come in?"

"Why, yes, yes, of course." Leonora moved aside.

"Thank you." Lady Cosgreave swept into the living-room. Leonora closed the door hastily and followed her.

"Would you like some tea? Or a drink?" It was later than she had thought. "Do sit down."

"Nothing, thank you." Lady Cosgreave remained standing. "I just wanted a quick word with you. For your own good."

"Again?" This concern for her welfare was touching, but Leonora had learned to suspect it.

"You've been confiding in Annabel," Lady Cosgreave accused. "I tried to warn you about that. Before you even moved down here, I tried to warn you."

"That was why I came to be here under false pretences," Leonora said bitterly. "As a grieving widow."

"Annabel has been upsetting Molly. I've just come from there. Molly was in tears. I will not have my friends badgered because of your delusions."

"Now wait a minute—"

"Annabel would believe you because she wants to believe you. She's always fancied herself as a Miss Marple." Lady Cosgreave smiled unpleasantly. "One day of Annabel's gin consumption would lay Miss Marple out under the table for a month."

"Annabel is *not* an alcoholic!"

"Did I say that she was?" Lady Cosgreave raised an eyebrow. "I am merely warning you—again—that Annabel likes to ferret out everyone's little secrets. More serious, is what she does with them once she knows. Ever since her debutante days Annabel has supplemented her income by selling items to the gossip columns."

"What?"

"They pay quite well, I understand. I've often thought Annabel ought to give me a commission. She's made enough out of me over the years—although she doesn't know I know that."

"Annabel? I don't believe it!"

"Your belief does not alter the facts." Lady Cosgreave shrugged. "There are still people who believe the earth is flat."

"But—" It was beginning to make horrible sense. Leonora remembered the relish with which Annabel had said, *"Dinah is one of the best-documented women of her generation"* and *"Her life is an open gossip column."* It seemed that Annabel had good reason to know.

"I shouldn't like Cosgreave Hall to make the gossip columns again," Lady Cosgreave said. "If we do, I'll know who to blame. I've already had a word with Annabel. She'll behave herself this time; she likes living here. As I believe you do."

Leonora nodded, speechless. Another veiled threat? Lady Cosgreave seemed to specialize in them. Perhaps she deserved having her escapades revealed to the gossip columns—she might be even worse without a threat of her own hanging over her head.

"I was sure we could come to an amicable understanding." Lady Cosgreave smiled. "Now then, come to dinner tomorrow—seven-thirty."

"I don't really think—"

"And I quite agree with you. However, Bunty thinks it would be best if you were there. You've met nearly everyone—it will be basically the same group as last weekend, with just a few visiting foreigners. Bunty says Tessa and Phil have already been inquiring after you. If you and Annabel aren't there, it will look quite pointed. We'll expect you at seven-thirty."

"Well, if Annabel—" Surely, Annabel would not be able to resist what might be viewed as a gathering of the suspects. Leonora was curious herself.

"She'll be there," Lady Cosgreave said grimly, "and on her best behaviour." Her tone indicated that Annabel at her best left a lot to be desired. "I shall, of course, expect the same of you." Again, her tone bespoke little hope of getting it.

"I'll try not to swing from the chandelier," Leonora said with the new tartness Cosgreave Hall was teaching her.

"You know perfectly well what I mean. This weekend is quite vital to us. Eddie is signing an agreement that promises to bring in a fortune . . . eventually."

"Eventually . . ." Leonora echoed.

"Oh, there are risks, of course." Lady Cosgreave sighed,

then brightened. "But, as I've always told Bunty, what is life without a few risks?"

They had certainly taken enough risks in moving a dead body and concealing it. Their reason for doing so might just lie in these weekend gatherings and the anticipated fortune to be gained. But there was something about the way Lady Cosgreave had emphasized "risks" . . .

Leonora remembered that it was supposed to be axiomatic that there was a time in the life of every millionaire when, if the police had been called in, he would have wound up in prison instead of in *Who's Who*. Was this Eddie's time? No wonder he had been willing to go to such lengths to keep himself free from official scrutiny.

"Seven-thirty." Lady Cosgreave was departing. "And remember—your very best behaviour!"

James had been press-ganged, too. He stood alone in a corner of the drawing-room, twitching. Inadvertently, he met Leonora's eyes and looked away again quickly.

The scorched drapes had been replaced, Leonora noticed, not with new ones but with different ones, probably borrowed from another room as a stopgap measure for the weekend. The table was still in its new position, a Paisley shawl thrown over it, fringes sweeping the floor and completely concealing the burned carpet.

If only James didn't look so hangdog, the whole episode could be forgotten. Certainly, none of the weekend guests appeared to be thinking about it. The scraps of conversation Leonora heard all around her were to do with big deals in the City, the movement of the Market and the currency, prospects for a Dawn Raid on an unnamed company next week; they were all so caught up their own concerns that a minor fire a week ago was already ancient history.

Annabel was in the far corner, hemmed in by the Oink and actually managing to smile and look interested in what he was telling her. On her best behaviour, indeed. Leonora was relieved to see her, having tried since last night to telephone her and getting nothing but a busy signal. She had been forced to the conclusion that either Annabel had taken her receiver off the hook, or there was an epidemic of out-of-order telephones. Annabel glanced in her direction just then and raised her glass in salute.

Leonora raised her own glass and continued looking around for familiar faces. They were all there—or almost all. Molly and Giles were riding herd on Eddie over by the doorway; he was obviously keeping his escape route clear, determined not to be cornered by Annabel again.

Dinah was in gracious converse with two City-types Leonora did not remember having seen before. Bunty was circulating, with Phil in attendance and Tessa trailing them just a step behind.

Only Clio was missing and, just as Leonora registered this, she appeared in the doorway with a distinguished looking unknown male in tow. She firmly guided him past Eddie, not even allowing him to pause when Eddie stepped forward to greet him, and brought him over to Leonora.

"You haven't met Tom!" she announced triumphantly. "I've been telling him all about you. Tom, this is Leonora!"

"How d'you do?" Tom shook hands briefly and unenthusiastically. Leonora got the impression that, whatever Clio had told him, he had not been listening.

"Leonora is our new neighbour," Clio said brightly, perhaps suspecting the same thing. "In the gardener's cottage."

"Yes, yes," Tom said absently. "I'm sure you'll like it here. If you'll just excuse me—" He made a sudden move backwards and to one side, detaching himself from Clio. "I really must speak to Eddie."

"But you've just got back—" Clio clutched at him but he eluded her. "You have all week to talk to Eddie."

"Won't be a moment." He gave Leonora an insincere smile. "Sorry, but it's quite important." And was gone.

"Oh dear," Clio sighed. "I did so want him to myself for just a little while."

"When did he get back?" Leonora asked quickly. A deep flush was mounting in Clio's cheeks and she looked as though she might burst into tears.

"This afternoon. Quite late. He barely had time to change for the party." Clio was regaining her composure, but her attention was still centered on her husband.

"Has your telephone been repaired yet?" Leonora tried to keep the conversation neutral as Tom reached Eddie and was immediately drawn to one side while Giles and Molly were waved away as though they were intrusive servants. Giles's mouth tightened with annoyance.

"This morning. Of course, it was too late then. Tom had given up and stopped trying to call. So it was a lovely surprise when he just walked in."

"What a shame they couldn't have repaired it earlier." If Tom had really bothered trying to call, that was.

"Yes—" Clio frowned slightly, perhaps catching the shade of criticism in Leonora's tone. "Actually, Tom *was* coming home at just the time he promised—but Eddie telephoned him and sent him off on some sort of secret mission. He wouldn't even tell *me* what—" She gave a light laugh that didn't quite come off.

"I don't really *mind* Eddie hijacking my husband, but I do think he might have told me he'd done it. He *knew* I was expecting Tom home a week ago. He should have known I'd be worried—" Clio's voice quavered, tears were perilously close again.

"Eddie has a lot on his mind—"

"So he should!"

Leonora blinked. For an instant, Clio had sounded spiteful and quite unlike her usual sweet self.

"Oh dear, I'm sorry." Clio tried to pull herself together, "I know poor Eddie's health is failing. We must be tolerant and—Excuse me, I really must speak to . . ." Clio darted away, tears glistening.

Leonora let her go. Tom, deep in conversation with Eddie, did not even notice as his wife dashed past him in distress.

"Bunty says I'm to take you in to dinner." James had appeared at her side. "If you never want to speak to me again, I'll understand, but I'm afraid we must sit beside each other at dinner."

"I'm not angry with you, James." Leonora was relieved to see the glass of Perrier water in his hand. "Let's forget the whole incident."

"All very well for you to say. Forgive and forget, eh? But you'll never really forget, will you?"

"You *do* make yourself memorable." He had asked for that. In a curious way, it seemed to comfort him.

"At least you're not pretending it never happened. That's what the others do, you know. Makes me feel like the invisible man."

"You're not the only one. The way Tom Warriner treats Clio, she could be the invisible woman. Maybe there's something in the atmosphere around here."

Something in the atmosphere, indeed. It even affected those who didn't live here. Tessa and Phil sat opposite Leonora and James at dinner; Leonora could not avoid overhearing bits of their more private conversation.

" . . . think you might have rung. It was your idea in the first place." It seemed Tessa was another one who was feeling invisible. "And there I was, stuck with the tickets."

"Gee, honey, I'm sorry. Something came up and I forg— Uh, I wasn't able to get to a phone."

"What happened to your cellphone?"

"Oh, er, it was back in London."

"And you were down here. You seem to spend most of your time at Cosgreave Hall these days."

"You know the deal Eddie's setting up. It takes a lot of time and preparation. Once we've got this settled, I promise you, things will be different.''

"Oh yes?'' Tessa's quick glance towards the head of the table said that was just what she was afraid of.

"There's a risk to everything, mind you—'' On Leonora's other side, the Oink was braying on. "But you've got to take risks in the Market, in life, in everything.''

"I suppose so,'' Leonora agreed absently. Where had she heard that credo before?

"I'm advising my clients to put everything they have into it. Even if they have to raise a second mortgage. This opportunity will never come again—and it's practically foolproof.''

"Umm-hmm.'' It had better be, if he had anything to do with it.

"I may say, Eddie is behind us one hundred percent.'' He amended, "One hundred and twenty per cent.'' He paused and looked at Leonora hopefully. "If you'd like to come in with us, I just might be able to manage a place for you. Tight squeeze, though. So many want it.''

"Don't bother,'' Leonora said. "I'm an impecunious artist, remember?''

"Oh, right!'' He looked startled and then lost interest. He turned to his partner on the other side and didn't bother wasting another word on Leonora for the remainder of the meal.

Across the table, Tessa and Phil seemed to have run out of verbal communication, too, but their body language was eloquent. Phil was leaning away from Tessa, awaiting an opportunity to speak to Clio, who was on his other side and seemed to be caught up in a duologue with one of the visiting foreigners.

Conscious of something vaguely awry, Leonora looked farther along the table and found Tom sitting between Lady Cosgreave and Annabel, about as far away from Clio as he could possibly get.

"Excuse me?" Leonora turned back to James, who had muttered something too low to be distinct.

"Pepper," he repeated. "Please pass the pepper."

"Certainly." She looked for the little solid silver peppermill she had been admiring earlier, but it was not in sight. "Sorry—it must have gone down to the other end of the table."

"It doesn't matter," James said. "It was just a sudden whim. At least—" a wintry smile flickered on his lips—"they haven't served oysters tonight."

"Just as well." She shared the brief amusement, glancing automatically toward Eddie. He looked hale and hearty enough, thank heaven. She began to cherish a faint hope that they could get through this evening without anything untoward happening, but the previous record of events at Cosgreave Hall did not encourage too much optimism.

For the moment, all was going well. Leonora saw Bunty surveying her guests with satisfaction—and also keeping an unobtrusive watch over Eddie. At one point, Bunty casually slid the butter dish just out of his reach, giving rise to the suspicion that Eddie was going to be put on a healthfood regime once the weekend was over.

Annabel had noticed the gesture, too, and Leonora met her eyes, intending to exchange a smile over the situation, but Annabel was unexpectedly frowning.

Curiously, Leonora looked around the table again to see what was disturbing Annabel. Everything appeared to be in order. Unless she objected to the fact that Clio's partner was eating his dessert with the wrong implement, but she hadn't thought Annabel was that snobbish.

The maids began serving coffee. Leonora was vaguely surprised but, with so many people, of course it was easier than serving it in the drawing-room. It also appeared that the ladies were not going to be called upon to withdraw and leave the gentlemen to their port and cigars tonight. Presumably because the old-fashioned custom would not sit well with the female City high-fliers present tonight. Tessa apart, there were several women who had not been here last week—and they were of a different breed.

Eddie was flanked by, and paying court to, a pair of women of indeterminate age with cold rapacious eyes and harsh New York accents. They would not take kindly to anything that implied they were of lesser worth than their male colleagues.

Yet, somehow, the party seemed to be dividing anyway. Those with financial interests became dominant, their conversation so cryptic that the others could not follow it. Leonora did not particularly wish to; she continued her desultory conversation with James, who, she discovered, could be quite amusing whenever his inferiority complex allowed him to be.

"I don't think some of you have seen my workroom—" Eddie pushed back his chair and his announcement caught Leonora's attention. She had not yet had the promised guided tour.

"If you'd like to look at it now," Eddie went on, "I think you might be interested. We can call up the closing prices on Stock Exchanges all over the world."

"Great!" "Brilliant!" The chorus of approval was almost drowned out by the clatter of chairs being pushed back as the weekend guests rose *en masse*. Eddie was definitely the Pied Piper of the evening.

"Oh, Leonora, dear—" Lady Cosgreave drew her back as she was about to follow the others upstairs. "Perhaps you could see it at a later time. There isn't a great deal of room up there and it will be crowded as it is. Anyway, I believe Annabel wants to speak to you. In the drawing-room."

CHAPTER 21

In the drawing-room it was clearly to be seen that there had been a deft separation of the financial sheep from the goats.

Annabel was standing by the fireplace talking to James and gave no indication that she had ever wanted to speak to Leonora.

Molly and Giles were sitting side by side on the sofa, casting nervous glances in Leonora's direction. They needn't have worried; Bunty was hovering protectively in front of them. No awkward questions were going to be allowed.

Tom Warriner had gone upstairs with the others, leaving Clio on her own as usual. Tom, in fact, had been in the vanguard of the move, immediately behind Eddie.

Clio now stood alone on the far side of the room pretending an absorbing interest in the small display of *objets d'art* on the corner whatnot. She looked lost and forlorn; again, Leonora felt a rush of annoyance at the unfeeling Tom.

Before Leonora could cross the room to join Clio, Lady Cosgreave caught her by the arm. "Do come and tell me more about your painting," she cooed. Firmly, she led Leonora to an unoccupied corner of the room.

"Now, I don't want you to be shy," she said. "You mustn't hesitate to tell me when you want me to give you the first sitting for your portrait practice. I have some free time next week."

"Oh, not yet!" Leonora said hastily, then wished she hadn't. The implication now hanging in the air was what she *would* do Lady Cosgreave's portrait—at a slightly later date. She had been outmaneuvered again.

Annabel suddenly glanced across at them, raised her eyebrows and sent Leonora a sympathetic look. The self-satisfied expression on Lady Cosgreave's face had obviously told her that something had just gone wrong for Leonora.

"Oh, Mummy—" Bunty came up, looking rather breathless. "May I speak to you for a moment?" She glanced at Leonora, then back at her mother, and moved away. "Outside?"

"Of course, Bunty." Lady Cosgreave rose and fixed Leonora to her seat with a piercing look. "You stay there," she commanded. "I'll be right back." She and Bunty moved off towards the door.

" . . . must talk to Eddie again . . ." drifted back over Bunty's shoulder just before the door closed after them.

Leonora sat there for a few minutes, during which Lady Cosgreave did not return. She began to recall that she did not have to take Her Ladyship's orders anyway. And hadn't she been told that Annabel wanted to speak to her? That should be excuse enough if Lady Cosgreave required any.

Leonora got up and went over to stand with Annabel and James.

"What has Dinah talked you into now?" Annabel greeted her.

"I'm afraid I'm going to be stuck doing that portrait," Leonora said gloomily. "There seems to be no way out of it."

"Go abstract," Annabel advised. "Tell her you're entering your Picasso Period and paint her with two noses and three eyes. That'll teach her!"

"Maybe." Leonora would not be cheered. "But it still means I'm wasting time on a canvas I'd rather not paint."

"Dinah takes advantage," James said indignantly. "She uses other people's weaknesses against them. You're too polite. You ought to tell her you won't do it."

"Threaten to send a bill," Annabel suggested. "That'll make her think again."

"I don't think it would work. She keeps telling me that she's allowing me to practice on her, as though she's doing me a favor."

"That's Dinah! All heart—and always to her own advantage. If you're going to live here very long, you're going to have to toughen up."

"I'm a lot tougher than I was when I moved in," Leonora said truthfully. Another few weeks here and she might get a lot tougher than she really wanted to be.

Already she had grown so tough she had forgotten poor Clio. Just like Tom—and everyone else. Guiltily Leonora looked across the room. Clio, still standing there alone, so fragile and vulnerable, was trying to pretend that she was absorbed in the beauty of the glass paperweight she had just picked up.

Leonora watched as Clio tilted the paperweight first one way, then the other, to let the light catch the depths and shadows in the embedded pattern.

Watched as Clio stared intently into the rounded glass surface... watched as Clio glanced swiftly around the room... watched—incredulously—as the antique paperweight suddenly disappeared into Clio's handbag.

"What is it?" Annabel had been alerted by Leonora's involuntary gasp. She followed the direction of Leonora's gaze.

Clio was standing there innocently, seeming lost in admiration as she stared down at the whatnot—which was now, Leonora realized, somewhat denuded of its display of treasures.

"Oh," Annabel said flatly. "I was afraid of that."

"You mean—?" Leonora stared from Clio to Annabel as another piece of the jigsaw clicked into place.

"No, don't worry, James." Annabel put her hand on James's shoulder, pushing him towards the sofa. "You go and talk to Molly and Giles. I'll handle this."

Leonora, still incredulous, followed her as she walked slowly across the drawing-room. Clio watched them approach, a faint half-smile on her lips. Almost challengingly, she picked up a small Victorian silver posy-holder and began examining it.

"A word with you, Clio," Annabel said.

"Yes?"

"Not here." Annabel led the way into the library, closing the door firmly behind them.

Leonora was still with them, but neither Annabel nor Clio said a word to acknowledge her presence.

"All right." Annabel held out her hand. "Let's have it."

Meekly, Clio handed over her bag. Annabel opened it and began emptying it on the library table.

The glass paperweight, a silver peppermill, a gold cigarette lighter bearing no familiar initials, a silver dessert spoon (no wonder her partner had had to use the wrong implement), an ivory fan. a soft leather tobacco pouch, a sapphire tie-pin, a pinchbeck-and-amethyst snuff box . . .

The pile of loot grew until Leonora wondered how Clio had managed to fit it all into one handbag.

"That's mine!" Clio stretched out her hand to repossess a diamond-studded gold locket and chain. "Tom brought it back to me from Switzerland." She smiled mistily. "He *does* remember me sometimes."

Silently Annabel allowed her to reclaim the locket, but continued to search the handbag for other pilfered items. A silver paperknife joined the pile on the table.

"Is that all?" Annabel asked sternly as the handbag yielded up no other treasures.

"I think so," Clio said dreamily. "Oh no, I almost forgot." She fumbled in her bodice and tossed an emerald bracelet on to the pile.

Leonora closed her eyes, unwilling to witness any more. There was silence in the room. When she opened her eyes again, Clio was standing by the door, holding her now-depleted handbag. The glittering hoard was still on the table.

"I'm terribly tired," Clio said. "I think I'll go home now. Would you make my excuses to my host and hostess, please?"

"Of course," Annabel said. "They'll understand."

"They always do, don't they?" Clio paused with her hand on the doorknob. "And you can tell Tom I've gone to bed—not that it will interest him. You can also tell him I don't want to be disturbed. That will suit him."

"I'll relay the message," Annabel said. Something in her tone suggested that she would add a few embellishments of her own.

"Oh, and Leonora—don't look so stricken. You were bound to find out, sooner or later. After all—" Clio gave a tremulous laugh—"if everyone was perfect, what would people talk about?"

The door closed silently behind her. Leonora and Annabel regarded each other quietly for a long moment.

"Well!" Leonora said finally. "No wonder all the trades-people deliver for her."

"That's how you train them," Annabel said. "If you don't care what happens to your reputation."

"How awful!" Leonora shuddered.

"Could be worse," Annabel said. "At least she's escaped prosecution—so far. I wouldn't like to think what tricks Tom has had to pull out of his sleeve to keep her out of Court."

"But—" Leonora remembered the way the Manager of Anselm's Department Store had hovered at Clio's elbow, subtly hounding her out of his store. "That day I went to High-marsh with her—do you suppose the store people thought I was an—an accomplice?"

"Don't worry about that." Annabel smiled briefly. "They know she's a lone wolf. In fact, she wouldn't have gained admittance to most stores unless she *had* had someone with her. You were a guarantee of her good behavior."

"I suppose there's no use saying you should have warned me—"

"No use at all. Anyway, as Clio says, you were bound to find out, sooner or later. Everyone knows."

"Everyone knows . . ." Leonora said thoughtfully. "Just as everyone knows about James. And I suppose—"

From somewhere upstairs, there came a horrendous crash. Then a high-pitched screaming began.

"Good God!" Annabel said. "What's that?"

They rushed out into the entrance hall. There was nothing to be seen. All the commotion was centered somewhere above them.

"Upstairs!" Annabel led the way. By this time, Molly, Giles and James were crowding behind them.

"The turret room—" Lady Cosgreave appeared as they reached the top of the stairs, jostling Annabel in the race to the next flight of stairs. "Something's happened up there."

"Eddie! Eddie!" The screaming was clearer now, rising above a background hubbub of excited voices. "He's had another blackout! He's fallen downstairs! Eddie—speak to me!"

Eddie lay at the foot of the narrow flight of stairs leading up to the turret. He was face down and they could not see whether or not he was still breathing. One leg was twisted out at an impossible angle.

"Blast!" Annabel said under her breath. "I knew he should have stayed in hospital where he was safe."

CHAPTER 22

"Take it easy, honey." Phil had a tight grip around Bunty's waist trying to hold her back as she fought to reach Eddie's side. It was only too obvious that she wanted to throw herself on him and shake him back to consciousness. "Take it easy, he'll be all right."

Eddie did not look all right. He lay there motionless.

"Oh, Bunty! Oh, my dear—" Lady Cosgreave pushed her way to her daughter's side. "And Eddie! Poor dear Eddie! What happened?"

"He fell downstairs." The Oink stated the obvious. "Don't worry, we've rung for the ambulance."

"He hadn't been feeling well all day," Bunty wailed. "I wanted him to rest before dinner, but he wouldn't. Now he's had another of his blackouts—and at the top of a flight of stairs! Oh, Eddie—"

"He still has a pulse." Kneeling by Eddie's side, Molly tried to be comforting. "It isn't too strong, but it's there. He's got a fighting chance if—" She cast a worried look at the twisted leg. "If everything else is all right." Surreptitiously, she slid her hand along his spine, checking it.

"Oh, Eddie—" Bunty still fought to reach him. Phil still held fast.

"Don't touch him!" Molly said sharply. "Phil, take her downstairs. Take them all downstairs. I'll stay here until the ambulance arrives."

"Sure. Come on, everybody," Phil called out. They filed down the staircase from the turret room, shuffling awkwardly, hurriedly, around Eddie's prostrate form.

"He *will* be all right, won't he?" Only Tessa paused to plead for reassurance.

"I don't know," Molly said.

"But—" The answer wasn't good enough. Tessa stared down at Eddie, horror in her eyes. "But he's *got* to be all right. He was fine just a few minutes ago, showing off his computer and laughing—"

"Oh, Eddie!" Bunty sobbed. She struggled against Phil's restraining arm. "Eddie—"

"Bunty, my dear, be brave," Lady Cosgreave said.

"Let's go downstairs with the others, honey," Phil encouraged. "We can't do any good here."

"No! I'm staying with him. He's my husband!"

"Too bad you don't remember that more often," Tessa said, not quite under her breath.

"For God's sake, Tessa—" Phil was anguished. "Not *now*!"

"Eddie—" Distracted by Tessa, Phil's grip had loosened and Bunty twisted free. "Eddie—" She hurled herself forward to fall on her husband.

"Catch her!"

"Hold her!"

Annabel and Giles leaped to capture Bunty before she landed full force on the helpless Eddie.

"Steady on, old girl," Giles said.

"He mustn't be touched!" Molly crouched over Eddie, protecting him. "Can't you understand? We don't know how badly he may be injured. If he's shaken or jostled, it might kill him."

"Perhaps—" Tessa began in a small, cold voice, but met Annabel's warning frown and stopped.

"Downstairs!" Molly ordered. "All of you! Giles, see what's happened to that ambulance. Make sure someone really did call."

"Okay," Phil told Annabel, taking a grip on Bunty again. "I've got her."

Annabel relinquished her hold on Bunty and stepped back to walk beside Tessa as they followed the others downstairs. Leonora was right behind them. Last in line, she looked back over her shoulder to see Molly checking Eddie's pulse again and looking thoroughly worried.

"He wasn't ill," Tessa almost whispered. "He was fine, the meeting was going well, then someone called him outside. It was a woman's voice—"

"Don't say any more!" Annabel stopped her. "I'll talk to you later." She peered over the stair rail. "I hope no one heard you."

She was looking straight at Lady Cosgreave as she voiced the hope.

Leonora followed as they went silently down the remaining flight of stairs to the reception hall. Why would Lady Cosgreave want to harm her son-in-law? And could she have done so? She had been on the first floor when Annabel and the others had rushed up the main staircase.

And yet . . . had Lady Cosgreave been slightly breathless? As though she had been running even before she joined in their rush to the turret stairs?

But why Eddie? For that matter, why Horton? Leonora returned to the point that had occurred to her just before Eddie's fall. How could Horton have been blackmailing anyone here when they all knew each other's secrets?

Molly and Giles weren't fooling anyone about their situation. Leonora had seen the others trying to keep James away from that fatal one-drink-too-many. And every trader in the vicinity knew about Clio.

Exposure was the blackmailer's threat—secrecy the commodity he sold. Since everyone knew everything, there was no reason to kill Horton.

"Make way! Make way!" the Oink shouted officiously, opening the front door for the ambulancemen. "Straight up the stairs," he directed them. "All the way up. Brought a stretcher, have you? Good!"

"Oh, Eddie—" Bunty made one last attempt to break free and follow the ambulancemen before Phil and Giles managed to wrestle her into the drawing-room.

"She's hysterical," Tessa said. "Someone ought to slap her face." She sounded as though it had been an ambition of hers for a long time. Leonora was beginning to understand why Annabel had thought Lady Cosgreave ought to land Hereward before he discovered the state of play.

"Not now," Annabel advised. "You might get carried away and there are too many witnesses. We don't want you up on an assault charge."

To Leonora's surprise, Clio was sitting in the drawing-room, watching as everyone entered.

"Thought you'd gone," Annabel greeted her.

"I was at home when I heard the ambulance arrive," Clio said. "Naturally, I came back to see what was wrong. Eddie's taken another bad turn, I gather."

"You might say that." Annabel looked at her thoughtfully. "He's taken a header down the turret stairs."

"Oh, no! How awful! Is he . . . badly hurt?"

"I'm no quack," Annabel said. "At a layman's guess, I'd say he's going to carry a nasty limp for the rest of his life. And I wouldn't like to bet how long that might be."

"Oh no!"

Clio's consternation was touching to behold, but Leonora found herself viewing it jaundicedly. Clio had been furious—in her own quiet way—with Eddie for having hijacked her husband without telling her. And now that Leonora knew more about

Clio's quiet little ways of showing her displeasure, she wondered how far Clio might go. Had she ever left the house? Or had she slipped upstairs to stand outside the door of the turret room and softly call an unsuspecting Eddie out to meet her vengeance?

"Here they come!" From his sentinel point in the reception hall, the Oink called out the tidings.

There was a dignified mêlée as everyone tried to get back into the hall to see what might be the last of their host. Still imprisoning as much as supporting Bunty, Giles and Phil shouldered her to the front of the crowd.

Slowly the ambulancemen descended the staircase carrying their blanket-shrouded patient. A solemn Molly walked beside the stretcher, matching her steps to theirs, holding aloft a plastic flask attached to Eddie's arm by a long plastic tube.

The onlookers shuffled uneasily as the procession passed them. Some of the men reached upwards, then remembered they were not wearing hats; they shifted their gestures to an uneasy fumble with their neckties.

"Well," one of the New York women said. "There goes the ball game! Might as well get back to London tonight and see if I can connect with an early flight in the morning."

"I'm with you!" the other woman said. She appeared to have slightly more tact, however, for she glanced around and added, "We'd just be in the way here. There's nothing we can do. Except, maybe, send flowers—"

"Oh, Eddie!" Bunty shrieked.

As though that were the signal for a general exodus, the other weekend guests mumbled their condolences and fled to their rooms to pack their cases.

"I want to go with Eddie!" Bunty wailed. "I *must* be with him—"

"Later—" Phil took her back into the drawing-room and sat her on the sofa, still retaining his grip on her, as did Giles. "He's in the hands of the experts now. Back in Intensive Care. There's nothing you can do. You'd only be in the way."

"In the way! My Eddie! Oh, Mummy—make them let go!"

In the midst of all this emotion, there had not, Leonora noticed caustically, been any actual tears.

"It's best that you stay, Bunty." Lady Cosgreave was grim-faced. "Your guests are leaving, you must see them off. Later, we'll both visit Eddie in . . . in Intensive Care."

CHAPTER 23

It didn't take long to see the guests off. They left so rapidly, it was obvious that they felt the ship was sinking. Their perfunctory apologies and expressions of sympathy were dealt with by Lady Cosgreave rather than Bunty, who seemed to have lapsed into a trance.

When the last car door had slammed and the last motor revved up and faded away down the drive, some of the nervous tension in the drawing-room evaporated. Lady Cosgreave collapsed abruptly into the nearest chair as though her legs would no longer hold her; she looked grey and drained—and considerably older.

"Get me a drink, Annabel," she gasped.

"Drinks all round, I should think." Annabel looked at her old friend with concern and motioned James and Giles towards the serving tray to do the honours.

"Thank you, Annabel." Lady Cosgreave accepted the drink that had been thrust into her hand and opened her eyes. "Thank you, *James*." Her eyes widened, she looked around. "Annabel?"

"I'm over here, Dinah." Annabel had moved away, distancing herself from her friends.

"Annabel—" Dinah pleaded. "Come here and let me talk to you."

"Too late for that, Dinah, I'm afraid." Annabel looked sad, so sad. "I'm afraid it was probably too late a long time ago."

"No!" Dinah said. "No! Let me talk to you." She looked around at the others, frowning. "Let's go outside—"

"Mummy!" Bunty said petulantly. "Mummy, everyone's gone now—" She ignored the people still surrounding her. "Let's go and see Eddie. I want to go now!"

"I think not," Annabel said.

"We can work something out—" Dinah was still pleading.

"Er, perhaps we ought to leave," James said. He motioned hopefully to Giles, to Clio and Tom, but they paid no attention. Wild horses couldn't have dragged Leonora away at this stage either.

"It won't make any difference," Annabel said. "You might as well stay."

"Mummy!" Bunty tried again. "You *said* we could go and see Eddie."

"Do you really think he'll want to see you!" Annabel asked.

"Of course he'll want to see me. If—" Bunty's face crumbled. "If he *can.*"

"Annabel—" Dinah pleaded.

"Your mother's tired, honey," Phil said. "I'll drive you down to the hospital."

"Oh yes," Tessa said, even more sadly than Annabel. "You'll take care of *her*, won't you?"

"Look, Tessa, this is business," Phil said, with a trace of desperation. "You know the whole deal falls through if Eddie—" He shot a nervous glance at Bunty and broke off.

"It's fallen through anyway," Tessa pointed out. "The others have gone back to London and scattered. They may not be too keen to try again after this."

"Do you mean . . ." Dinah was pale. "The agreement wasn't signed?"

"We were just getting to it," Phil said, "but suddenly Eddie made an excuse and left the room. The next thing we knew—we heard the crash as he fell. That finished it!"

"Oh no!" Dinah slumped. There went that fortune.

"It might be just as well," Bunty said. "I was never so sure it was such a good thing." There went all the risks, too, and she was obviously glad to see them go.

"You were always against it, weren't you?" Tessa asked.

"It always seemed to me that Eddie was risking too much." Bunty looked around the beautifully-appointed room. "Not all of it his." She was not quite the risk-taker her mother thought she had raised.

"But you don't have to worry about that now, do you?" Annabel looked at her strangely.

"Probably not." Bunty could not quite hide a smile. "Of course," she added quickly, "Eddie may still have this bee in his bonnet when he comes home, but I hope I'll be able to persuade him against it."

"All it might take," Annabel said slowly, "is just a little push in the right direction."

"Yes—No—" Bunty lost all traces of a smile. "What do you—?" She broke off, not wanting confrontation. "I'm sure he can be persuaded," she said. "After he's had more time to think it over."

"*If* he survives," Annabel said. "In which case, he'll have more to think over than his financial deals, won't he? He may turn his attention to some simple arithmetic: like adding up two and two."

"Annabel, please—" Dinah made one last despairing effort to stop her old friend.

"Listen," Phil interrupted, "I don't know what's going on here, but I don't like it. Bunty's had a nasty shock—she doesn't need you bullying her on top of it."

"Listen to Sir Galahad!" Tessa gibed bitterly.

"Now why make a crack like that?" Phil turned to her. "You've got your hooks into Bunty all the time lately."

"Just as she's got her hooks in you!"

"Come on—" Phil put his arm around Bunty. "We don't have to stand here and listen to this. Let's go!"

"Before you go," Annabel said, "it might be a good idea to telephone ahead and find out if Eddie has recovered consciousness. If he hasn't, you may be all right—for a little while longer. But if he's been able to talk, you might find the police waiting for you."

"What the hell are you talking about?" Phil glared at Annabel.

"Bunty knows." Annabel nodded to her. "Horton died wearing another man's cast-off shoes. It will be very interesting to see—when his body is dragged out of the river—if he's wearing one of Eddie's discarded suits."

"He will be." Leonora remembered that Annabel had not been present when Molly had admitted that she had at first mistaken the body for Eddie's—and why. "He was wearing Eddie's old tweed suit."

"I thought I hadn't seen it lately—"

"What body? Who the hell is Horton?" Phil's voice rose. "What *is* all this?"

Leonora understood now—and was glad she was not going to be the one to have to explain it to Phil. How do you tell a man that he has been responsible for inspiring murder? Certain that Phil would marry her if she were free, Bunty had been trying to kill her husband all along. After killing Horton by mistake, she had tried—and failed again—the night of the dinner-party. If Eddie was still alive tonight, he would know what she had done and be able to link it to the other attacks. Bunty would have had to come out into the open to push him downstairs. It was her bad luck that such a fall was not necessarily fatal. But Bunty was an opportunist, as she had shown all along.

"Annabel—" Dinah moaned. She had known—or feared—the truth herself. "We keep telling you—there *was* no body."

"Wasn't there?" Annabel turned to Giles. "Are you going to continue this charade—now that you've seen where it's led?"

"No." Giles was pale. "No, I'm not. It's no use, Dinah. This has gone too far."

"And it wasn't the accident you thought it was," Annabel said.

"No." Giles looked straight ahead, not meeting any eyes. "In the light of these new developments, I no longer believe it was."

"What accident?" Phil was still bewildered, but more subdued.

"Tessa hit our ex-gardener as well as our gatepost last week." Bunty was still in there fighting. "It was rather naughty of us to hide the body—but we wanted to protect her."

"That's a lie!" Tessa said. "I didn't hit anything but the gatepost. And I only hit that because I'd swerved to avoid hitting an animal."

"Naturally you'd say that." Bunty dismissed her protest.

"Horton—" Annabel spoke over both their heads to Phil— "was the ex-gardener. He was sacked before you appeared on the scene, so you never met him. I believe you're familiar with his cottage, though. It's the little place across the river. Quite convenient for a tryst—if you don't mind a dead man's bed."

"What?" Phil's arm slid away from Bunty's waist.

"You're all mad!" Bunty pouted. "And my poor Eddie perhaps lying dead." She moved off towards the library. "I'm going to ring the hospital and find out how he is."

Dinah started after her, but Annabel shook her head. Dinah stood irresolute outside the library door. They could hear dialing sounds just before Bunty said, "Hello—?" and closed the door.

"That's why you were in *my* cottage—" Leonora remembered Phil's embarrassment and wild story. "You thought you were meeting Bunty there. But I'd moved in and she hadn't had a chance to warn you.''

''You startled me,'' Phil admitted. ''But—'' he looked uneasily at Tessa—''let's not go into that now.''

''You needn't worry about me,'' Tessa said. ''I know she's been your mistress for ages. That's why you're always down here. If Eddie hadn't been so trusting—''

''He'd be a lot better off tonight,'' Annabel finished for her.

''I'm sorry about this,'' Giles apologized to Leonora. ''I'm afraid we've put you through some uneasy moments. But we thought we were acting for the best.''

''So you threw the body into the river.'' Annabel shook her head. ''Did he really look like an accident victim to you?''

''Head wounds,'' Giles said vaguely. ''Molly and I discussed it. It was possible—''

''The thought of a blunt instrument never crossed your mind?''

''I'm afraid we weren't thinking very clearly at the time,'' Giles admitted.

''You certainly weren't,'' Annabel sighed.

''Don't blame Giles,'' Molly said. ''It was all my fault. I talked him into it.''

''I was willing enough.'' Giles caught her hand and held it tightly. ''Don't blame yourself.''

''That's all very well,'' Annabel said, ''but whatever possessed you to turn yourselves into accessories after the fact?''

''We didn't think of it that way.'' Molly looked startled. ''We just wanted to help Bunty and Eddie out of a difficult situation. And then . . .'' She hesitated.

''And then?'' Annabel prompted.

''We'd have done it anyway, but then Bunty promised to tear up our IOUs from the bridge games—''

''We should have smelled a rat then,'' Giles said. ''But the losses had been mounting rather high and the offer was welcome. Apart from anything else, the repairing lease keeps us strapped. The guttering needs replacement and I don't like the look of a crack that's appeared in the corner of the ceiling and—'' Giles shrugged. ''It seemed almost fair, considering what the upkeep of the East Wing has cost us.''

''Eddie was quite upset about it,'' Molly said. ''He hadn't realized we'd been playing for money—or how much . . .''

The sound of a car motor cut through the silence. Annabel dashed to the window, the others crowding behind her. They saw the car hurtle down the drive at a dangerous speed.

Leonora held her breath until it had cleared the gateposts and shot away. After all, Bunty had been the biggest risk-taker of them all. She had played to inherit Eddie's fortune, undiminished by commitments to a new financial cartel; she had also hoped to gain another fortune by marrying Phil. And she had lost the game.

''Bolted!'' Annabel said. ''What else could one expect?''

''She won't go after Eddie, will she?'' Tessa asked anxiously. ''She's already tried to finish him off once tonight— right in front of us! If Phil hadn't caught her before she fell on him—''

''I don't think she'll try again.'' Annabel went over to the library and opened the door. A buzzing noise directed their gaze to the telephone receiver lying on the table as though it had been thrown down in a sudden panic.

''No, it looks as though Bunty has had bad news. Eddie must be alive—and talking. She won't go near the hospital. They'll be on the lookout for her.''

''My poor baby,'' Dinah said. ''What will she do now?''

''She'll keep bolting—until they catch up with her,'' Annabel said. ''I suppose we ought to see if her passport is missing.'' She sat down on the sofa. No one else moved.

''No,'' Annabel agreed with a sigh. ''We'll leave that to the police. I suppose they won't be long in getting here.''

''I shall get the best legal—and medical—advice available.'' Dinah sank wearily down at the other end of the sofa.

"Thank heaven there are sufficient funds. Since Eddie didn't sign that agreement—" She broke off abruptly, remembered why he hadn't signed it.

"I—I hope Eddie will want to help," she said uncertainly.

"I should think Eddie would want a divorce," Annabel said. "He shouldn't have any difficulty getting custody of the children—in the circumstances."

"Poor Bunty," her mother sighed. "She's made a hash of her life again."

That was one way of putting it, Leonora thought. Bunty hadn't done a lot for Horton's life, either. Or for that of the other people whose lives had been bound up with hers.

Phil looked stunned, just beginning to realize that he had had an affair with a murderess; that it was the affair that had turned her into a murderess. Later, he might even begin to realize what Bunty's plan had been—and what he had escaped.

Tessa watched him quietly but made no move towards him, not even when he blindly stretched out a hand towards her for comfort. She was going to have a lot of thinking to do before she decided whether they could ever get back on their old footing.

"Annabel—" Dinah said.

She could paint them, Leonora thought suddenly. A double portrait, just as they were now, sitting side by side, with the weight of years and experience in their resigned faces.

"Annabel, will the newspapers have to know?"

"I'm afraid so, Dinah." Annabel sighed deeply. "But they won't find out from me."

THE END